THE DEAD OF THE HOUSE

The Dead of the House

A NOVEL

BY

HANNAH GREEN

B·O·O·K·S & Co.

A Turtle Point Press Imprint

NEW YORK

B·O·O·K·S & Co.
TURTLE POINT PRESS
New York

© 1996
Hannah Green

First published in hardcover by Doubleday & Company, Inc.
Most of the contents of this book appeared originally in
The New Yorker © 1966, 1969, 1970 in different form.

Design: Christine Taylor
Composition: Wilsted & Taylor Publishing Services

Library of Congress Number 95-080864
ISBN 1-885983-07-7

For

My Mother

Mary Allen Green

and

In Memory of My Father

Matthew Addy Green

1901–1967

Contents

I have tried to write, seemingly, a very real book, which is, in fact, a dream. I got the idea from life, but I have proceeded from vision. I have made use in equal parts of memory, record, and imagination. Members of my family and other people I have loved, my feelings about them, and theirs about one another and many other things as well, have provided the inspiration, the starting point, for this novel, but the characters in this book bear no more relation to their real-life counterparts than the characters in a play bear to the actors when they have left the stage. The historical personages mentioned, including the early members of the DeGolyer family, are, of course, real, but the others are fictional.

ONE

In My Grandfather's House

I N THE YEAR 1840 my great-great-grundfather, the Reverend Mr. Nathaniel Nye, who was then the minister of the Baptist Chapel at Barnoldswick in the West Riding of Yorkshire, received a call from God to go to the New World, and go he did.

"You know the story of how it happened, don't you?" my grandfather asked me one afternoon when I went to visit him and he was alone in his house of old red brick with its white columned porch and high gambrel roof with attic dormers. His yard always looked a bit woodsy and wild on Salt Lick Avenue, a street of fine old gray stone mansions from the turn of the century and a newer variety of large white house in an American Tudor style, all but Grandpa Nye's with smooth lawns and clipped hedges.

I did know, but I said I didn't because it was a good story and I wanted to hear him tell it.

He sat, as he always did, in his green velvet chair at his desk in the long dark library, and he spoke in a voice warm and hoarse and full of tones—like the word "yesteryear," I thought when I was a child.

"My grandfather," he said, "was born November 15, 1815, at Barnoldswick in the West Riding of Yorkshire, the son of Samuel Nye, a tanner. My grandfather told me that his father, Samuel Nye, was scandalized by the conduct of the village parson, who rode to hounds and daily finished off two to three bottles of port and was put to bed dead drunk. So Samuel Nye left the Church of England and joined the Baptist Chapel, and it was in the Baptist faith that his sons were reared.

"Now, this Samuel Nye was also scandalized by the conduct of his own father, boon companion of the parson and, like him, a mighty drinker. And my Grandfather Nye had no recollection of his Grandfather Nye except of seeing him once dressed in a red uniform and mounted on a white horse in a parade of the Duke of York's Regiment. He had been brought up to have the idea that his grandfather was a person of reprehensible habits, but he had the greatest respect for his father, who, he said, was a most worthy man, and he spoke with pride of his brothers. There were in the family seven sons, and each of them when he attained to man's estate was more than six feet in height and weighed more than two hundred pounds.

"In the year 1840 my grandfather came to Canada, and the manner of his coming was this: He was the minister of the Baptist Chapel in Barnoldswick. One of its members, Mr. Moreley, a great friend of Samuel Nye, had some years before emigrated to Montreal. There he had prospered. He returned to Barnoldswick for a visit and on his first Sunday in his old home he went to church and heard my grandfather preach. At the conclusion of the service Mr. Moreley said to my grandfather, 'In the New World they are hungering and thirsting for that kind of preaching.' Grandfather went home and told my grandmother that he had received a call from the Lord to go to America. My grandmother, a woman of vast common sense, when he explained the exact nature of the call, poohpoohed the idea, saying that Mr. Moreley had intended only a gracious compliment. But my grandfather would not listen to her objections. It was a call from the Lord, and go he would. So in less than a fortnight the family was packed up and in Liverpool, ready to sail. There were then three children—my father, Joab, the eldest, who was three, and my Aunt Mary, and Uncle Benjamin. In Liverpool a great misfortune befell them. Little Benjamin fell ill and lay for weeks at death's door. They were delayed there for three months, a delay that all but exhausted my grandfather's savings, but at last little Benjamin was well enough to sail.

"In the New World my grandfather prospered. He was in every way better off than he had been in England. For seventeen years he was the minister of the Baptist Church at Sherbrooke, in the Province of Quebec, and there were born Samuel, James, Victoria, and Frederick. All these save Frederick reached maturity. Frederick died as a baby, and Grandmother and Grandfather grieved over him for many years. Grandfather never spoke of this baby without tears in his eyes. I had the great happiness of knowing these grandparents intimately and of seeing them often.

"When it came time for his sons, Joab and Benja-

min, to go to McGill College in Montreal, my grandfather moved there so as to be with them. He became
the agent of the British Bible Society, a position he
held until old age made him give it up.

"He was a large, well-set man and, after the fashion of his day, he wore whiskers—a full beard,
snowy white, which gave him the air of a patriarch.
He was a man of strong character and a most affectionate disposition. When my Grandfather Nye's
mind was made up, nothing could change it. He was
devout and earnest, a good preacher and a good
mixer. In his work as agent of the Bible Society, he
traveled a great deal and he had a new audience in
every place. That is a great advantage, for a man can
repeat an address time after time and in the process
of repetition it becomes polished. He had an address
on the Armada which I had the pleasure of hearing
twice. It was a fiery philippic against the Catholicism
of Spain, and a glorification"—Grandpa Nye spread
out his arms as he said "glorification," and repeated
it—"and a *glorification* of Protestant England under
Elizabeth."

Then he said, "Vanessa, my dear, would you like a
cigar?" It was our private joke. I always said, "Yes,
thank you, Grandpa Nye," and I took one, and bit off

the end, and lit it, and puffed great clouds of smoke, and he said with resignation, "You take after your pirate ancestor on your Grandmother Nye's side of the family."

And my cheeks burned with pleasure.

"Oh, tell me more stories," I said.

"Very well," he said, "I'll tell you the story of how we came to Cincinnati, and then . . . and *then* I'll tell you about the first DeGolyer to come to the New World.

"My Grandfather DeGolyer was, like my Grandfather Nye, a Baptist minister. He was of old American stock. In the years of 1859 and '60 he had business in Montreal and removed there with his family. Thus it was that my father met Vanessa DeGolyer, and the two were married on January 1, 1862."

Grandpa Nye then told me the story of his own boyhood and their move to Cincinnati very much as I read it in *Memories of My Boyhood*, which, along with *The Nye Family Record* and *Summer Wanderings in Northern Canada*, he had written and privately printed and bound in red leather and inscribed "To my dear sons." I set the story down here just as he wrote it in *Memories of My Boyhood*:

"Mother and Father were gentle, loving, and companionable. They took an immense interest in their children. They attempted at all times to forward our ambitions, and to assist us in the things we wished to do. They made every sacrifice on our account. To me their memory is precious.

"For the first ten years of their marriage Father taught Latin—first in Brockville, later at McGill. So it was that Ben and I were born in Brockville, Nora in Montreal. I was born December 4, 1862, and named Nathaniel John—Nathaniel for my Grandfather Nye and John for a little uncle, Mother's only brother, who, had he lived, would have been only six years my senior. He was a fine vigorous boy, the idol of his elder sisters. The winter before I was born he fell on the ice while skating, fractured his skull, and died from the injury. Ben was born January 30, 1864, and named for Father's brother, Benjamin; and Nora, born May 5, 1866, was named Honora Lawrence for my Grandmother Nye's beloved sister, whom she left behind in Haworth near Barnoldswick in the West Riding of Yorkshire. Of this Great-Aunt Honora I know only that she had a lofty character, and that, like the Brontë sisters, she loved to walk on the heathery moors. She died unmarried in the thirty-ninth year of her age before my grandfather and

7

grandmother returned to England to visit for the first time.

"In the summer of 1871 we took a trip by steamer over the Great Lakes to Chicago. It was a splendid trip. We went to visit Mother's Uncle David Lee DeGolyer, a wealthy contractor who made his fortune cedar block paving Chicago. He drove down Wabash Avenue to his office with a fine span of horses. Later his name was linked, through no fault of his own, I am sure, with the *Crédit Mobilier* scandal. He had Garfield as attorney, and in the campaign of 1880 the Democrats made capital out of the so-called DeGolyer Swindle. They used $329 as a campaign slogan, that being the amount paid Garfield by David Lee DeGolyer.

"Then we went to Joliet to visit Cousin Harry DeGolyer. While we were in Joliet, President General U. S. Grant came through town. He spoke from a platform at the back of the train, and then he kissed all the small girls, including our Aunt Eda who was seventeen.

"It was on that trip that Father first met Uncle George DeGolyer who was visiting from Cincinnati. Uncle George was Mother's first cousin as well as the husband of her sister Jenny, and he was half

owner of a firm in Cincinnati that made carriages—
Queen City Carriages. He had sixty-three first cousins. He was a rich man by the time he was twenty-
five. He was evidently well impressed with Father,
for he said to him in the typically expansive De-
Golyer fashion, 'Come on down. Business is good,'
and he offered Father a position in his firm. I think
that Mother was anxious to be near her sisters, and
Mother and Father undoubtedly thought there would
be more opportunities for us in Cincinnati. At any
rate, the following year Father gave up his teaching
and we removed to Cincinnati.

"As clearly as if it were yesterday, I remember the
day early in May of 1872 when we arrived in Cincinnati from Montreal, having come on the Erie Railroad. We arrived on a Sunday morning. The day was
warm, a delightful spring day. It was in great contrast
to the cold we had left behind in Montreal. Apparently we arrived unexpectedly, for there was no one
there to meet us.

"We walked down Fifth Street to the river and
crossed on the ferryboat, the *Fanny Webster*, to Ludlow, where Uncle George and Aunt Jenny lived. Father and Mother were tremendously impressed by
the foliage and the flowers. Everything was in the

fullness of its spring beauty. In the yard of the house that Uncle George had rented for us there were four apple trees, all in bloom. As we stood on the bank of the river, Father looked out amazed to see that the Ohio was such a small stream. In comparison with the St. Lawrence it did not show to advantage. At that time Ludlow was a lovely village. The Southern Railroad had not been built; there was, of course, no railroad bridge, and the town was a charming place with fine old mansions with their slave quarters. Mother had a colored woman who had been a slave for a servant. She did not know how to read or write or count money.

"I was nine when we arrived in Ludlow. Our residence there gave a turn to all my life after, for it was there I acquired my love for the water. The riverbank in Ludlow was a boy's paradise. The river was our playground. All day long Ben and I were in the water or on the wide sandbar that stretched westward in those days from Ludlow to Bromley. We played with the shanty-boat children and helped the shanty-boat men pull in their nets of fish. Often there were a hundred to the catch—catfish, dogfish, buffalo, river perch, and gar pike.

"We went naked and were brown as Indians. We

10

took to the water as naturally as ducks. We became absolutely amphibious. There was a great deal of traffic on the river in those days. Our greatest joy was to swim out to the huge log rafts that drifted down the river. We clambered aboard and floated downstream, listening to the talk of the rivermen, listening to the creaking between the logs. We dreamed of the wide Mississippi, of Cairo, of Memphis, New Orleans, and the Gulf. Then after a mile or so we dove from the raft and swam ashore and made our way home along the sandbar among the hundreds of soft-shelled turtles.

"Perhaps Father and Mother feared we would grow up into river roustabouts. The shanty-boat people had a bad name, but as far as I know we came to no harm by our association with them. At all events, in 1874 we moved to Walnut Hills. Walnut Hills was not then what it is now. Beyond Locust Street the open country began. The people of Walnut Hills were generally of a better class than those of Ludlow. Father and Mother soon made congenial friends.

"Ben and I soon made friends with three fine boys, Duff Hatch, Eugene Stewart, and John Hoffman. We spent all our spare time together. We made splendid expeditions through the wilds of Bloody Run to Sandy Bottom, a swimming hole just below where my house is now.

"Many of the experiences of my middle years are dim and misty, but my memories of my boyhood are as clear and vivid in my mind as if they happened yesterday. Often as I walk in my woods now, there returns to my mind the heated joy of afternoons spent swimming, and walking, and climbing trees in the wilds of Bloody Run in the days when Bloody Run was a lovely stream of clear water, full of fish, and the forest was, some of it, still the original forest. We boys found arrowheads and knew we roamed the hunting grounds of the Indians.

"I still feel the great weariness of rowing the good skiff *Ulysses S. Grant II*, which we hired at the Marine Dry Docks at the foot of Kemper Lane, up the river to the Little Miami on our first camping trip. We rowed up the Little Miami to a point about a mile from the mouth, where we came upon a great stump, ten feet tall and six feet in diameter, the melancholy remains of a forest giant, and there we made camp. The Big Stump Camp, we named it. If ever boys were happier than we, I doubt it. All day long we climbed up the stump and dove from it into the water. We

12

went barefoot. We were in the water so much we didn't bother to dress. We caught fish and explored the area, going as far as the Ohio, where we lurked in the willows looking out at the traffic as the Indians had in former days. It was our ambition to be as nearly savage as possible, and in this spirit we formed the L F B M, the Lively Five of the Blue Miami, and tattooed our manly bosoms with our initials and the skull and crossbones."

My sister Lisa and I always knew about Grandpa Nye's tattoo, but we saw it only once, one day in 1936 when he came to visit us just for the day at Neahtawantah, on the West Bay of Grand Traverse Bay in Michigan, where we always went for the summer.

I remember we were at West Bay on the beach and Daddy was crouched beside Lisa and me to show us where Grandpa Nye was—way out on the glassy bay, a zigzag spot moving through the heat, the sun, the green jelly glare of the bay, which smelled of stones and fish. He'd paddled in Uncle Harry's red canoe out to the Island, which was far away, wooded and green—a rounded hill and a long, low tail. No one lived there except the eagle. Mama, who was lying on her towel, said enthusiastically, without opening her eyes or lifting her head, "Children, this is going to go down in history."

As we waited for Grandpa Nye to come back, we could hear water-dream voices—people talking way down the beach. "You see," said Daddy, "we can barely see them, but the lake, when it is a mirror, reflects their voices to us in somewhat the same way that it reflects the image of the Island." He put his glasses in the little linen bag with his cigarettes, hung it on the juniper bush, and went in for a brief swim.

When Daddy came out of the water, Mrs. Black called down from the pavilion, "Morgan, you look exactly like Mahatma Gandhi in those trunks." Minnows, silver slips in softened sunrays, swam near the dock, and I put my ear down in the water in the little stones to listen.

Then Grandpa Nye came in close and we could hear the water dropping from his paddle between strokes. He brought the canoe high up on the sand. His blue eyes were vague and he had in his skin the odor of the sun's heat and the cool green odor of the lake.

We saw the thin white scars of his tattoo and we touched his leathery chest. We touched the L F B M, which stood for Lively Five of the Blue Miami and looked like the letters Daniel Boone cut on that tree down in Tennessee:

D. BOONE
CILLED A BAR
ON TREE
IN YEAR 1760

We touched the skull below the letters, and the crossbones below the skull.

Grandpa Nye moved his fist down across the L as if he were cutting it. He tightened his lips. "We cut with penknives. The we rubbed in gunpowder to make it last," he said.

"*Gun*powder," Lisa and I said. "Really?" We looked up at him.

He made a great sweep with his arms. "Lisa and Vanessa," he said, "did you know that long ago before the glacier this was all the bottom of a great salt sea?"

We did know, we said.

I smelled the odor of the lake and the sun in Grandpa Nye's skin and I saw scratches on his legs. I had the feeling he and I were somehow the same person. I knew he'd been walking barefoot in the forest on the Island, and he'd heard a branch cracking way off in the hot still woods and felt the heavy wings of the eagle close overhead. "Did you see the eagle, Grandpa Nye?" I asked.

"Yes," he said, "I saw the eagle." Then he went into the water to swim and he swam side stroke straight out toward blue water. "Papa swims a mile every day in the summer," Daddy said. "He always swims straight out because if anything should happen, he wants . . ." Daddy broke off, and when, finally, Grandpa Nye came back he went under water and came up with two Petoskey stones, one for Lisa, and one for me.

Later when Grandpa Nye was very old, when he was over ninety, I imagined how in his mind sometimes as clearly as if it were yesterday the warm Miami flowed nearby, and he and Ben and Duff Hatch and Eugene Stewart and John Hoffman danced around the fire and whooped like Indians. Duff Hatch looked up at the noon sun and said, "I swear secrecy to Gitchie Manitou." And Ben said, "I likewise." They sat around the fire and dipped their penknives in the flames and they said, "We swear brotherhood." Then they began to cut the letters onto their chests—the L, the F, the B, the M. He couldn't remember the pain, just how hard it was to keep going, just how they went on all together; blood was on their chests and the endurance became a strange pleasure. When they cut the skull and cross-bones, he said, "*La Belle Dame sans Merci*," and he thought of the pale lady who was death, singing in the river. "Now that it may last our lifetimes," he said, and Ben said, "Yea, yea," and they all said, "Yea, Yea," and they took the cool ashes they called gunpowder and rubbed them into the cuts and they lay back to dry out their tattoos. The sun and the sky and the high grass and the red of the Indian paintbrush swam in his eyes with the pain that flashed, as he remembered it years later, like a pale light in his chest, and he remembered also how after they moved to College Hill there were five girls—the Washburn twins, Laura and Maude, and the Friendly twins, and Miss Alice Powell—who claimed that L F B M stood for we Love Five Beautiful Maidens, and so they took the beautiful maidens on a picnic to the Big Stump Camp on the Little Miami. And he remembered he was standing with Laura Washburn on the riverbank near the dark stump whose root reached down into the river and Laura had on a white dress and he said,

"*La Belle Dame sans Merci*," and he looked at her pale face and the color rose into it, and he looked at her round green eyes. Her skin was cool as the air deep in the forest, and the air was absolutely still.

In *Memories of My Boyhood* Grandpa Nye said, "So that we boys could go to Farmers' College, the family made its final removal to College Hill in 1878. There we found an ideal society. Father and Mother met people of culture, and we found boys and girls who were the best of companions. Uncle George and Aunt Jenny made their home with us. The house in which we lived was spacious. It was set in a plot of eight acres; half was orchard. There was a stable and a henhouse and a carriage house. We bought a cow when Andrew was born, February 2, 1879, and I had to feed and milk it. This was not task work, for I found pleasure in it. I raised pigs and made quite a bit of money selling the increase. We raised nearly all the vegetables we ate. We had an abundance of apples, pears, grapes. Mother and the aunts used to peel and quarter the apples, which we boys put out on the low roof of the kitchen to dry. Green corn was cut from the cob and dried the same way. We had an acre of lawn, which we let grow until the grass was high. Then it was cut with a scythe, cured, and the hay was served for winter feed to the cow. Of course we had no central heating or running water. On Saturday night we had a bath in the kitchen in a washtub in front of the stove. Nothing unusual about that—everybody did it.

"On College Hill during the last years of his life, Father took up amateur photography—there was a great craze for it then—and this gave him infinite pleasure. There was in the fore part of our cellar a spring and a little pool in which milk and butter were kept, and Father carried the water of this spring into his darkroom—an arrangement of which he was proud.

"My first year at Farmers' College was under the presidency of Reverend John B. Smith, a mild-mannered old Presbyterian minister who had mastered the art of chewing tobacco without expectoration. We boys were fascinated by this remarkable accomplishment. He was succeeded by the late P. V. N. Myers, a great scholar and a great teacher. He was an inspiration to us. He made us love reading, and he had many distinguished guests who did us good. Among them was Bronson Alcott. Mr. Alcott was a philosopher, Plato and Socrates in his own person. He remained for almost three months at the college. Daily we sat at his feet. He talked and talked—such marvelous talk—a stream of gold forever flowing from his lips. Sometimes he spoke of his Concord neighbors, Emerson and Thoreau. Of course he had an immense influence on us. He was a vegetarian, and I resolved to follow his example. For many weeks I ate no meat. Mr. Alcott always referred to it as 'flesh.' But finally I fell from grace. The dear old man had only one failing—he could not endure being referred to as the father of Louisa May Alcott. He thought *Little Women* a trifling performance, whereas his philosophy was concerned with the eternal verities. He was an impressive and venerable man, and his appearance carried weight. He looked to be what he was.

"We were also visited by Alfred Russel Wallace, the co-inventor with Darwin of the Theory of Evolution. He made all of us evolutionists at a period when many men believed that to believe that doctrine was to imperil one's immortal soul."

THE DEAD OF THE HOUSE

In *The Nye Family Record* Grandpa Nye wrote, "In 1886 I married Laura Washburn, daughter of E. W. Washburn, Principal of Hughes High School. Mr. Washburn, like my father, was a Latin scholar, and he was the author of an excellent Latin grammar. We were married in his residence on College Hill, and we went to Washington and to Old Point Comfort and Richmond, Virginia, on our wedding journey. We went to Richmond because it had been the Capital of the Confederacy, and most of all because there the Libby Prison was situated. Libby Prison had such fame even as late as 1886 that I wanted to see it almost as much as I wanted to see the Capitol at Washington. In Washington we called on President Grover Cleveland at the White House, and in Richmond on Governor Fitzhugh Lee, who put his carriage at our disposal that we might better see the city.

"Five children were born to us:

Charles Washburn Nye—April 12, 1887
Nathaniel John Nye—December 2, 1889
Joab DeGolyer Nye—January 28, 1891
Edward Benjamin Nye—February 12, 1892
Morgan Burke Nye—May 15, 1901

"My little namesake died July 3, 1897. He was a beautiful child and of exceeding promise. Joab was a man grown when he died, August 25, 1914, and he was a writer of verses with a great future before him, for he had ability of the first order."

Among the many photographs that hung in the upstairs hall at Grandpa Nye's there were a number of pictures of Uncle Joab, and often I stopped to look at his large-boned handsome face. In one of the pictures he was standing on the rocks at Pointe au Baril and his hands were on Daddy's shoulders when Daddy was about eight and he was seventeen. Uncle Joab had a look of great strength and ease and buoyancy. Once Cousin Cato, when I asked him about Uncle Joab, said, "His poetry was a side of him you wouldn't have guessed. What you saw was how he loved the physical side of life. You saw it in how he paddled a canoe, in how he swam. He did it with such . . . such . . . gusto."

I kept the volume of Uncle Joab's poems by my bed at home, and I read him. I thought perhaps I took after him, and I liked him better than Rupert Brooke. He lived for a year in Harlem after Princeton, and then when he became engaged he returned home and worked on the *Enquirer*. "He loved newspaper work," Daddy said. "Just the way Papa did. That last year of his life he used to come home after midnight and read and write poems until it was almost light. I think he knew every line Poe ever wrote by heart, and he kept Poe's raven above his bedroom door. In the afternoons before he went back to the paper he used to play with Buggs and me. I was twelve then, I think. Buggs—Buggs was the great dog Buggs, an abandoned Indian dog; we found him on a camping trip."

Two months before his wedding day, Uncle Joab died. It was late that same August the First World War broke out. He went to the hospital to have a hernia patched up. He was so big and strong, the ether didn't put him under. So they gave him gas. The gas didn't do it, so they gave him more ether. Then they gave him chloroform. Sometimes I saw him lying strapped down on the operating table with the white-masked doctors bending over him, administering the anesthetic that killed him.

When we were at Grandpa Nyc's, Lisa and I went upstairs together and walked around the upstairs hall and looked at the pictures. We passed the many rooms—Daddy's room when he was little, Uncle Charles's and Uncle Edward's and Uncle Joab's rooms, and Grandpa Nye's office where he wrote *Old Tippecanoe: The Life and Times of William Henry Harrison*. We stopped to look at the picture of Grandpa Nye as a handsome young man. We stopped to look at Daddy in a long white dress going down the sidewalk in the days before the gingko tree was planted. We passed the portrait of little Nathaniel which hung at the head of the stairs. Up there he stood in his white sailor suit, wearing white shoes and socks, his skin pale olive, his eyes greenish, his hair dark and curly. When I was little he seemed to me big and frightening like an older cousin, and at the same time my mind was drawn to him, to the roses in his cheeks, for his skin contained that secret—death. "He died of diphtheria when he was eight," Daddy said. "That was before I was born, you know. My older brothers were devoted to him."

Little Nathaniel remained in my mind older than I, taller, until one afternoon when I was a woman grown (I was twenty-four like Uncle Joab), I looked up from the landing on the stairs and saw with a start how young he was, how little, a child of seven. Below me Grandpa Nye, his shoulders bent, walked slowly across the front hall, his feet scraping the rug, and I remembered twenty years before when his back was straight and he seemed stonelike and remote to me, he stayed with me alone a while. He took me on his lap and put his arms around me. "Today was my little Nathaniel's birthday," he said. There were tears in his eyes.

Lisa and I went by the couch in the alcove where Daddy was put when he was born in May, 1901. Daddy said, "I was eleven months in the womb and was born then by unusual means, somewhat in the manner of Macduff. The surgeons who operated on my mother in the house did not expect a live baby. No preparations had been made for a live baby. Turning out to be alive, I was placed on the couch that belonged to Frederick Funston Nye, the cat, and I was left there without attention while the surgeons were busy fixing up the patient. The story is that I was nursed by Frederick Funston and I was in good shape by the time anyone else could give me attention. Don't swallow this story, but there must have been something in it."

Uncle Charles told me Grandmother Nye wouldn't see Daddy for weeks. She wanted a girl. She raved. She was through, she said, with having children. She hated to hear him cry.

Daddy remembers Frederick Funston as an enormous cat who sat on Grandpa Nye's left shoulder at dinner when Grandmother Nye wasn't there. Frederick Funston liked to come down before anyone else in the morning and lick the butterballs smooth and take chunks from everyone's cantaloupe when they were in season. "Fritz was a *character*," Daddy said. "He slept with me."

Those were the days when Uncle Charles and Uncle Edward and Uncle Joab used to play Digging Panama Canal with Daddy. They made Daddy be the shovel. He hated that game. "Poor Daddy," I said to Lisa as we passed the couch.

There were no pictures of Grandmother Nye, and I never saw her until, when I was eight, I saw her in her coffin. Before that I thought, or half thought, she was a ghost up in the attic. Once when I was four, John, my oldest cousin, took me up the dark narrow attic stairs to show me Grandmother Nye's ghost. There she was in the gray light over by the dormer window—an enormous green cat nearly three feet tall, with a round lady's face. "Go away," she sighed.

When I saw her in her coffin, she was in the gold drawing room where usually no one went, although it was a perfect room done in gold, with graceful stiff-backed chairs of gold brocade. The fireplace was made of white and beige tiles, and a rectangular mirror was built into the blond wood over the mantelpiece. "My mother," Daddy told me, "used to come down and go in there wearing white gloves 'to receive.' She cared a great deal for such things ... whereas Papa did things in a natural way." After a moment Daddy said strangely, "I don't remember anything happy ever in that room." Uncle Charles told me he still could hear Daddy's screams coming from that room when Grandmother Nye had him circumcised at the age of twelve. "It was one of her crazy ideas," Uncle Charles said. "Circumcision had come into fashion then. The poor kid screamed in the night after that for a long time too. It didn't heal properly, and he was in terrible pain at certain times."

I remember we went to Grandpa Nye's and there were many people there, and Grandmother Nye was in her coffin in the gold drawing room. I went to look at her and I felt an awful closeness to her. I had a sense of the being, the life in her dead body. She was like a doll, only an old-lady doll, all in white. Her thin mouth was lavender white. Her old skin was a filmy lacquer over the roses in her cheeks, but behind her eyelids she knew something; she smiled faintly. I thought I was meant to kiss her.

27

Mama put her hand on me, and I didn't like Mama's hand on me. I went back into the hall where people were milling around in their overcoats in the cold morning light. Grandpa Nye was saying, "She was an unhappy woman in this life, Morgan." His voice was damp and tired.

Little Auntie Maude, Grandmother Nye's twin, was crying. Lisa said, "Don't cry. Death is like going to sleep." Auntie Maude took tiny steps every which way; tears glazed her old yellow cheeks, and her big bulldog chin was shaking. "Just like going to sleep," Lisa said.

Everyone, and Uncle Charles especially, was angry because Miss Janice wouldn't come out of her room upstairs, and Olympia in her black uniform was going up to get her. Miss Janice was Grandpa Nye's housekeeper. She was slim, with a full bosom. She wore chiffon blouses and was very pale. In fact, her skin was so translucent that her freckles seemed to be blue. I followed Olympia and went around into the alcove in the hall upstairs. Olympia knocked at the door. "Miss Janice," she said. "Miss Janice . . . They say they want you down there, Miss Janice." After Olympia was gone, Miss Janice opened the door. I heard her breathing in a strange fast way.

Then without shutting the door all the way she went back into her room. I didn't mean to look in, but when I went by her door I saw her in the mirror of the white bureau looking at herself. She took up the hand mirror and turned to look at her profile, then moved close to the mirror until she almost kissed her own pale lips.

I went down the back stairs and through the kitchen, and when I was out back I was crying. The ground was beating against my forehead and the cold grass was on my tongue.

When I went in again, the people were gone. Lisa said, "Olympia is going to give us lunch."

I went into the drawing room as far as the rug. I could smell the flowers still and the perfume from the coffin. I thought there were many dead people in the house, and I could feel the musty oldness of everything, the dust in the unused corners, the gray light in the thin back staircases, the closed-off rooms, the great dark attic where Grandmother Nye used to sit over by the dormer window. Now, I thought, all the dead would come to lie in their coffins with flowers all around and I would have to bend close; I would have to feel their noses with my nose and kiss their mouths.

29

Little Charles pushed me from behind right into the empty place where the coffin had been, and it was like bumping into her body. I felt it—cold, heavy.

"That woman upstairs is out to get us all," Little Charles said.

Lisa said, "Personally, I think Miss Janice is Bad Doo-Doo's sister." Lisa and I used to have dreams about Bad Boo-Doo and his brother Lee Roy. They lived in a long, low, gray house on the tracks down by the underpass.

Eugenie, who took care of us when we were little, told me years later that she remembered the days when Aunt Janice used to bring Grandpa Nye out to see us and drop him, then come back later on and pick him up. "That was in the early days when you was a baby, Vanessa," she said. "Mr. Morgan had a black heart for her in those days, so I did too. But later on he come to like her better. I did too. I always thought she was beautiful though. She was pretty as a . . . as a speckled pup. I'll never forget the day they was married," Eugenie boomed in her warm bronze voice. "I was over to your Uncle Virgil's. He brought me the paper. 'Look it here, Eugenie,' he says. It was on the *front* page."

I could remember Mama and Daddy coming back from what they thought was to be a cocktail party at Grandpa Nye's, and Mama saying she wasn't surprised—she'd noticed Janice calling him "dear" in front of people lately. Then they debated what Lisa and I should call Miss Janice now. Daddy said "Grandmother" was somewhat farfetched.

"That must have been about 1936," Eugenie said. "About a year after your grandmother passed on."

"Did you ever see her?" I said.

"No, I can't say as I did. They say she was . . ."

"What?" I said.

"Nothin', Vanessa."

I knew what she was going to say so I didn't pursue it. But I was always trying to find an image, a detail—something—so I would know what Grandmother Nye was really like. Usually when I asked what she was like, I got an image that would almost immediately be contradicted. In my mind only the memory of her dead body and my fear of inheriting her insanity grew.

When I used to ask Daddy or Uncle Charles what

she was like, their eyes would look hurt and, not looking at me, they would say, "Well, she was a fine woman. Very intelligent. Extremely gifted. She wrote some excellent papers on . . ."

Mama would say, "Nowadays they give women hormones when that happens. She would have been perfectly all right. You mustn't worry, dear; something like that is not hereditary."

Once Uncle Charles said, "She was never the same after little Nathaniel died." That was three years before Daddy was born. Daddy said once, "Maybe it was Joab dying."

Another time Uncle Charles said, "She was *always* crazy at a certain time of the month. I think Papa thought all women were like that, and he tried to ignore it."

Daddy said angrily, "She was always crazy." He used to have to go see her when she was in the sanitarium near Lansing, and after that when she went down to live in Biloxi. "She hated my father; she never would see him," Daddy said. "She couldn't trust anyone. She had to move all the time. Room to room. Floor to floor. Hotel to hotel."

And I saw my grandmother slowly aging, shriveling, her eyes moving suspiciously year after year;

always the Gulf winds, the rattle of palmettos, the voices upstairs talking about her.

"I can't have any pictures of her in the house," Daddy said. "It's embarrassing, but I can't. I'm sorry."

By the time I was old enough to realize there must have once been someone who was Grandmother Nye, who was the ghost in the attic, there were no pictures of her in Grandpa Nye's house either. But Kate, Uncle Edward's daughter, told me that once when she was there visiting and she was alone with Grandpa Nye, he told her that Grandmother Nye was a very beautiful woman. He got an old daguerreotype out of his desk drawer and showed Kate the picture of her grandmother when she was a young woman. I asked Kate what she looked like and Kate said, well, she looked like lots of old-fashioned women.

Charles (Little Charles) said he was taken to see Grandmother Nye in Biloxi when he was four, and he remembered her distinctly: she had bushy black eyebrows and was ill at ease with children. When I saw her in her coffin, she had a smooth, almost eyebrowless face, so I suspected Charles of mixing her up with John L. Lewis.

One afternoon when I'd been helping Grandpa Nye with the wine he made each autumn and we were both filled with the wonderful odor of grapes, he walked down to the car with me and right at the end of the walk he said, "Vanessa, have you got good legs?" I didn't know how to answer, and he said, "Your grandmother had beautiful legs." But when I told that to Daddy he said, "His memory is faulty. She had terrible legs. She had the worst legs in Cincinnati."

At a tea one time an old lady whose hand felt like a paper napkin fingering my arm said, "She was a lovely woman, my dear, perfectly lovely. We two taught Latin together at Hughes High School after we graduated. She won the gold medal and I won the silver." Cousin Kitty (Mama's cousin), who is the same age as Uncle Edward and used to go over to the Nyes' sometimes when she was in high school, said, "She was beautiful in a big-boned way. Her skin was fair and thin, it colored easily. She had a kind of grandeur. She was very gracious, very rich." But Daddy said, "She always wanted new horses, new carriages. She wanted to *drive* them faster. She was always after Papa for something."

And all the time my vision of her body in her coffin returned and caused in my consciousness all the dead of the house to unfold like white roses blooming where they lay in their coffins in the gold drawing room, each in turn, waxen, pale, surrounded by flowers: first little Nathaniel, the beautiful child in his small coffin; then Uncle Joab in his long, dark coffin —I could see his clear forehead and his mustache, and sometimes I imagined I could smell the ether that killed him; then Grandpa Nye's mother, Vanessa, who came to live in Grandpa Nye's house after Grandmother Nye went away, and died there in August 1918, in the seventy-ninth year of her age; and finally Grandmother Nye, so many years later, in 1935.

I was aware too of the calm, of the secret in their bodies when they lay in the gold drawing room, the secret they took with them into the dark earth, and of the last breathings, the restlessness, the desire not to die, which stayed behind in the house like the screaming of childbirth, like the screaming of Grandmother Nye going out of her mind that year after Joab died.

"Go up and shoot them, they're talking about me!" she screamed. Daddy and Uncle Edward went up to the attic with the gun. They could hear her screaming below, "Kill them, kill them!" After Edward fired the gun she was quiet. When they went back down she didn't say a word. Her face was puffed up with rage, her eyes were furtive, her body stealthy under her sheet, but she was perfectly satisfied. In the morning when Grandpa Nye came back from Knoxville, where the Morgan Burke Company had a lot of business, she started up again. "Keep him away from me, keep him away!"

About a month after that, Grandpa Nye stood at the door of the library in his high silk hat and his Prince Albert coat. He was going off to catch the night train south to La Follett, where at one of the blast furnaces owned by the Morgan Burke Company a man had been killed. (The first pig of iron out in the morning would be buried in the stead of the dead man.) "Good-bye, Morgan," he said. And Morgan (Daddy then when he was thirteen) sat in the library bent over *The Diary of Samuel Pepys*, which Grandpa Nye was reading him aloud after dinner in those days. "Good-bye, Papa," he said, but his father was gone.

He was not reading but was bent over the book trying to keep hold of himself for a few hours until Edward came back. He clenched his fists, put his head down in the book. He held his grief in his throat, and told himself, "Joab is dead. We will never see him again. Joab is dead."

36

He got up and went to the front door and called his dog. "Here, Buggs. Here, boy." Finally he heard him running from across the street. They went into the library and they both lay down in front of the fire. "Good boy," he said and kissed his dog's face, let himself be licked. Then he brought *The Diary of Samuel Pepys* to read in front of the fire. Then he got an idea. He stood up and proceeded as he imagined old Pepys would have done to the dining room, where he got out the port and a thin-stemmed goblet. "A quart of port and so to bed," he said.

Years later I said, "Did you *really*, Daddy?"

"I did," he said, pleased, and he told of the terrible night he spent. The room weaved and wheeled; he never spent such a horrible night. "'And those behind cried "Forward!" And those before cried "Back!" And backward now and forward,'" Daddy declaimed in the heroic style. In the morning he did manage to make his way up Salt Lick Avenue and get on the streetcar at Reading Road. But when he arrived at Hughes High School, Grandpa Washburn, who was the principal, passed him in the hall. "Grandpa Washburn got just one whiff," Daddy said, "and he sent me straight back home on the streetcar."

37

Of Uncle Joab, Daddy said later, when I asked him, "If *he* had only lived . . ."

He said, "I loved him more than any human being."

He said, "He was always so affectionate."

Late on winter afternoons as he showered and dressed after a hard day at his office, Daddy used to recite in his deep voice, "'I weep for Adonais, he is dead.'" There he'd break off and in a moment he'd say, "'O weep for Adonais, he is dead.'" Sometimes after a long pause he'd say, "'The soul of Adonais like a star . . .'" And there break off, while I, lying on my bed doing my homework, hearing Daddy, picked up Uncle Joab's book from my bedside table and opened it to

POEMS
by
Joab Nye
1891–1914

Privately Printed
Cincinnati
1917

38

and looked at the little picture of him in the front, which made me feel queer because, with his dark hair parted in the middle and combed back smooth and with his dark mustache, he looked old-fashioned, he looked like a soldier long ago in the First World War; he looked far away, unreal, who was so real to me I sometimes thought I remembered him.

And Daddy loved him, and he died—the one Daddy loved more than any human being died. The lump in my throat ached as if it would burst and my mind became feverish, and in this trancelike state I sniffed the sweet peeling leather of Uncle Joab's book and the musky perfume of the old pages, drew my fingers slowly across the paper that felt as if it were covered with a subtle cobwebby film beneath which the words were printed. "There come on leaden wings these dreams of sin," Uncle Joab wrote.

I read. I cut the pages. I came for the first time in all these years upon a poem from the lines of Virgil:

O quam te memorem, virgo? Namque
haud tibi voltus

IN MY GRANDFATHER'S HOUSE

Mortalis, nec vox hominem sonat—
O dea certe.

Uncle Joab wrote:

> All seems so fair and strangely sweet
> I whisper low in helpless love
> *O dea certe!*

"Fair blew the wind for Crete," Uncle Joab wrote, and it made me want to sing.

I held his book to me. I took after him, I thought. And here were his poems, and in my skin I remembered him, and when my throat became dark and full of blood, heavy and sad, and my mind burned, and a heavy airlike substance surrounded me, encasing me, when I said words then, they were the words of poems.

In the springtime I took Uncle Joab's book outdoors with me, and I put violets and spring beauties on it as if it were his gravestone. I lay in the grass and felt the soft air, the blossoms, the budding trees, the green things coming up from the earth where he was buried deep, and all those who died before him back to the first DeGolyer buried in the forest; and now the sweet presences in the air made me want to dance, dance until I would become all flowing hair, wind, voice, light, for the corn was little green shoots coming up from the earth, and sweet stems fluttered, and out of dark branches came buds like candle flames shining in the sun.

I got up and walked with Uncle Joab's book open and laden with violets and spring beauties. Light quivered in the stems and the petals. "'The soul of Adonais like a star,'" I said, and I felt the cool spongy grass under my feet.

That spring when Uncle Charles and Aunt Melissa came from Washington to visit, we (all but Lisa, who had dancing school) went to Grandpa Nye's to dinner, and after dinner, while I was standing by the high mahogany mantelpiece in Grandpa Nye's library in my white gold-threaded evening dress, Uncle Charles looked at me. Uncle Charles had a smooth handsomeness; he was like an ambassador. His skin was dark, his eyes were green, and he wore a tawny mustache that made kissing him good night a particularly delightful experience. He always smelled just faintly of bay rum with which he combed his hair.

"Vanessa looks like Aunt Nora when she was young, doesn't she, Papa?" he said. Aunt Nora was Grandpa Nye's sister.

"Yes, she does. She also looks the way I remember my mother looking when I was a small boy," Grandpa Nye said. "Vanessa, you bear a striking resemblance to both your great-aunt, Honora Nye Morrison, and your great-grandmother, Vanessa DeGolyer Nye."

Both Aunt Nora and my great-grandmother died a long time before I was born, and hitherto all I had known of Aunt Nora was that she was tall and dark and beautiful. She was Cousin Cato's mother.

In *The Nye Family Record*, Grandpa Nye wrote, "My mother was singularly gifted. She could paint, write, and act, and was withal a good mother and admirable housekeeper. All the DeGolyers had an artistic streak in them and they all loved to plan in a large way."

My great-grandmother was very dynamic, and after my Great-Grandfather Joab Nye's death she took to circling the globe. In an old scrapbook, I found a

42

postcard that she sent from Thebes in 1907 to Uncle Joab on the occasion of his sixteenth birthday. On the back of the postcard, my great-grandmother said she wrote to congratulate Uncle Joab on his mature age. "I was never so old as when I was sixteen," she wrote. "I am afraid I am too much in love with the Egyptian sun. I enjoy Arabic explorations." And she added that she was about to purchase in Luxor a long-interred cat for Grandpa Nye.

She was very loving, and one time when she was old and her memory had begun to fail, she came up to Grandpa Nye at a garden party. She put her old hands around her son's face. "I don't know who you are," she said, "but I know you are someone I love very much."

Grandpa Nye and Uncle Charles gazed at me fondly so the wine and the fire were hot in my cheeks and I felt a dizzy pleasure, a pride. I felt as if I were beautiful. I felt as if I were growing, harmonizing, settling into a form filled long ago in turn by these women, my great-grandmother and her daughter. They had been old a long time and had been dead now for many years. I didn't know how I was like them or what it was that made me quite suddenly appear to resemble them as they had been long ago, but it may have been the color, the vapor, the oil—whatever it was—that had come recently into my face, my skin.

In the warm library the gold firelight moved. The lights of flames and the dusky shadows brushed the surfaces of bronze statues, the dark-green linen walls, the oil paintings of forest scenes and harbor scenes, the gilt frames, the mahogany bookcases with glass doors, and the leather-bound books, the gold lettering. The shadows floated over the dark globe of the world, and the fire flashed in the green eye of the leopard Uncle Andrew shot in India. Andrew, the leopard, was tawny and wild stretched out on the long table under the bronze bull. I wished that I might look quickly and see in one of the dusky gleaming surfaces the reflection not of my face but of Aunt Nora's or Great-Grandmother's face in my face.

Grandpa Nye and Daddy and Uncle Charles went back to their talk. They were drinking coffee and Cointreau. Grandpa Nye was smoking his cigar, and they were discussing the Battle of Fallen Timbers. Grandpa Nye gave Daddy and Uncle Charles some facts about the battle they hadn't known before. He had followed the march of General Wayne's army step by step—by car, of course—going north along the course of the original road Anthony Wayne cut through the forest. "Mad Anthony Wayne was anything but mad," Grandpa Nye said. And to me he said, "The Indians called him Black Snake, which they esteemed as the wisest, the most watchful, and the most careful of creatures."

"The date of the Battle of Fallen Timbers, Vanessa, was August 20, 1794," Uncle Charles said, looking at me sternly for the moment.

Daddy and Uncle Charles and Grandpa Nye returned to their talking, but they continued to look at me from time to time, and I felt the grace of possessing a quality not mine but given me by the strange accidents of time, of blood, of love. In Uncle Charles's love for me there was the recollection of the love he felt for his aunt when he was a little boy and she was a young woman, and in Grandpa Nye's love for me there was the recollection of the love he felt for his mother when he was a little boy and for his sister when he was a young man. In loving me they were old men loving a young girl of their blood, and also young men, little boys, loving a grown woman of their blood.

Mama was talking to Aunt Janice and Aunt Melissa. "I don't know what we're going to do about Vanessa," she said. "She per*spires* so. It goes right through the shields. She ruins *all* her evening dresses."

The fat worm wrapped around my brain, shut out my breath, the light, squeezed water out onto my hands. My underarms were dripping, cold. Mama reached out to pat me when I went by her chair going out of the room. I hated her hands. I hated her to touch me. I couldn't stand it. I wanted to scream. When I was in the hall, I looked under my arms. The white and gold of my evening dress were turning to gray green.

I went upstairs and into the room where Grandpa wrote *Old Tippecanoe: The Life and Times of William Henry Harrison*, and where on top of the papers on his desk was his prism, catching gleams of light and transforming them. I picked up the prism and stood holding it, humiliated. I wanted to throw it through the window and break out into the clear cold night and go down into the woods beyond Grandpa Nye's back wall, over the stile below the woodpile and down through the night past the tall oaks and the sycamores, down through time to the little stream, Bloody Run, way down the hill in the valley of the

46

woods, where Grandpa Nye swam when he was a boy and the Ohio and the Big Miami and the Little Miami and Bloody Run were sweet warm streams full of sunlight and fish; and there in a grove of beech trees, which had been there even in the days of Daniel Boone and were a part of the original forest, I would bend down and find, gleaming in the dappled sunlight, an Indian arrowhead.

When Grandpa Nye had finished telling me the story of his boyhood on that afternoon I visited him and we were alone, Olympia came softly into the library, bringing us tea.

"Thank you, Olympia," Grandpa Nye said.

"Miss Janice is still downtown," Olympia said, "but she'll be home right soon."

I poured the tea and passed Grandpa Nye the bread-and-butter sandwiches. Then Calvin was at the front door and I went to let him in. Calvin was the West Highland terrier that Grandpa Nye and Aunt Janice got on their wedding trip to Scotland. His nose twinkled on my shins and he smelled pink and raw, like the flesh I could see through his shaggy white coat because ever since Aunt Janice got him she had washed him three times a week in Dreft. Once Daddy said, "There's no *dog* left in him." Grandpa Nye gave Calvin a bread-and-butter sandwich and told him to lie down and be a good boy.

"I was going to tell you about the first DeGolyer to walk in the American forest," Grandpa Nye said. "I was going to tell you about the forest then, and the Indians, and about the work of being a pioneer, but there is not enough time left today.

"The name of the first DeGolyer was James. He was born in France and he came to Canada as a soldier in the French army about 1748, shortly after the peace of Aix-la-Chapelle. He did not fight with Montcalm on the Plains of Abraham, for he was an American by the time of the outbreak of the French and Indian War. He was married to Jane Hatch, daughter of five generations of New England farmers. (Through her, your Uncle Ben has traced our ancestry back to William Palmer who arrived on the *Fortune* in 1621—the first boat after the *Mayflower*.) And so this James, our French ancestor, fought on the British side in the French and Indian War. He was a scout, stationed in the region of Lake George. Of course, you remember hearing about the time he was captured by Indians, don't you?"

48

"I do," I said. "But not really. Tell me." I could remember Uncle Andrew long ago bending down and telling me the story when I was still quite small, sitting in one of the child's chairs by the fire, listening to the wonderful talk. The story had made my bottom tingle, and ever since, when I thought of this remote ancestor of mine, I remembered his bloody wrists.

"That story survived the years," Grandpa Nye said, smiling. "There is an old DeGolyer manuscript that tells all about it and much more besides. I'll read it to you some day. This James and four of his sons are on the lists as soldiers of the Revolution. Even before Burgoyne marched south from Ticonderoga they had shouldered their hunting rifles and joined the local militia. They fought in the Mohawk Valley where the war of the Revolution raged fiercest. James and his son Joseph fought on the bloody battlefield at Oriskany where the Americans were victorious against Joseph Brant's Indians and the British. Another of his sons, James DeGolyer, Jr., achieved a certain fame for he was stationed at West Point and he guarded the spy Major André, and loaned him his Bible on the eve of his execution.

"After the Revolution, Joseph, the third son of the first James DeGolyer and our direct ancestor,

49

chopped his farm out of the forest at Fonda's Bush, later called Broadalbin, in the State of New York, raised a large family and became a man of substance and standing in the community."

Grandpa Nye stopped talking. He smoked his cigar, and was absorbed in his thought. As I looked at his old face lit by the green lamp on his desk, it seemed to me that he was sad suddenly. I looked at his thick white hair and his long leathery cheeks, his long hooked nose, and at his mouth, which was worn and old and wet and tore me up with feeling for him.

When I was little, I thought he looked like Tecumseh—like the dark engraving of Tecumseh that illustrated the essay he wrote on Tecumseh somewhere in a set of brown leather volumes called *Famous Heroes and Statesmen*. Once an old man bent down and said to me, "Your grandfather as a young man was lithe and handsome as an Indian. There was no other like him in Cincinnati."

Looking at him, I wondered and asked, "Grandpa Nye, do you think maybe we have Indian blood in us?"

He didn't hear me. "Shall we bring in some wood for the fire?" he said.

"Oh, yes," I said.

50

We got our coats and went through the dining room and the dark-wood pantry and the big dark kitchen and out the back door. When we were down by the woodpile, I started to ask him again, "Grandpa Nye, do you think maybe we have—"

"No," he said. I looked at his blue eyes, and he was looking out into the woods. "But we've a wildness in us and a love of the wilderness that makes us think we must be Indians. For me the great events of my life were my canoe trips in the Far North, when I made my way through the wilderness as the Indians had in early days. My last canoe trip was in the summer of '28, when we went from Norway House at the northeast end of Lake Winnipeg to York Factory on Hudson Bay. It has since been a great sorrow to me that . . ." he said, and broke off.

At home I had a little leather-bound volume of poems Grandpa Nye wrote, called *Cedar and Spruce*, published in September, 1918, and in the dedication Grandpa Nye said, "These verses were written for my sons, who, like their father, love the wilderness. This year these dear boys of mine are in France fighting their country's battles and could not go on a canoe trip in the country just south of Hudson Bay. To please them I have made a little volume of these verses of the wild woodland, as that was the easiest way to send them 'over there.' "

Daddy was still too young to go to war, and in a poem called *To My Son Morgan* Grandpa Nye wrote:

> I've crossed life's middle line
> The morning hours are thine
> And when I play with thee
> Thou givest thy morn to me.

Grandpa Nye selected some small logs from the woodpile and he gave them to me to carry. "Is that too much?" he said.

"Oh, no," I said.

"You have the wildness in you," he said. "It worries me."

Happy, I carried in the wood from the branches of trees Grandpa Nye had felled himself in his woods. He chopped the logs and split them. He was famous for his skill with the ax. "None of us could keep up with him," Daddy said. When Daddy was little, he used to go along every Saturday afternoon when Grandpa Nye went with his wheelbarrow into the woods below his house to chop wood. On the way out Daddy rode in the wheelbarrow which Grandpa

Nye pushed. On the way back Xerxes, the colored man, carried Daddy like a sack over his shoulders.

For many years the sound of Grandpa Nye's ax could be heard in the neighborhood, and when he was very old and no longer able to chop wood, in his ninetieth year and after, he could still be seen on certain afternoons in the old hat he wore around the place in spite of what Aunt Janice said, and in his woodsman's coat, walking slowly down Salt Lick Avenue with his wheelbarrow. Calvin, who was also very old, walked slowly along beside him, and waited when Grandpa Nye stooped down to pick up twigs and fallen branches for his fire.

Other afternoons, taking one of his favorite canes, Grandpa Nye would go out the back door and down and slowly up over the stile into his woods where he walked among the giant oaks, his feet shuffling through the leaves, his old hand reaching to touch the bark of a tree, the voice of his wandering mind occasionally speaking. "Oh, my dear boys," he said. "My sons."

Summer Afternoon, Summer Afternoon

O N HOT EVENINGS in early June when the sunshine was butter in the maple leaves across the drive, I would be upstairs trying to do my homework and Lisa would be downstairs at the piano, practicing. I wanted to be outdoors smelling the grass, playing the way we used to play —running, screaming, falling in the grass until the grass and the mud and the smell of evening blended and a train came and filled the air with its huge, warm rumble. I decided to go down and help Mama set the table.

In the hall at the foot of the stairs Lisa was playing

Finlandia, which Daddy loved, and behind her on the stairs Daddy sat listening. Lisa's dark, long-fingered hands moved over the keys. ("She has the touch," Mama said.) Her wide back was straight. She played and Daddy sat listening in his white summer ducks and white shirt, his head tipped back and to the side, his eyes full and liquid with joy and pain, his mouth loose, smiling. His face was perspiring, and around him was the smell of his shower, his cigarettes, his gin. "Bright Western Land," Lisa played.

I went by, the breath in my heart that made me hollow, helpless. I went on out to the kitchen. I wanted to be like Lisa. I wanted to play the piano the way she did; I wanted to be the way she was swimming in Grandmother Marston's pool, the water shining on her body, on her mouth, dripping from her arms, her hands, her curved fingers, as she breathed and turned into the water. I wanted the boys to like me; I wanted to be popular like Lisa. "What silver do we need tonight, Mama?" I asked.

She looked around. "Vanessa, humor Mama. Tuck in your shirt."

I looked down and saw my shirt tail was half out of my blue denim school-uniform skirt. Lisa came into the kitchen. Daddy was pacing back and forth in the dining room. "Dum dum dum dum," he sang ("Bright Western Land"), and when he came into the kitchen he was happy, moving his hands as if he were playing the piano.

He poured his gin over in his little liquor corner by the sink. He drank the gin, filled his glass with water, drank that and stepped out onto the back porch. From there he surveyed the neighborhood. Kroupa was down sniffing around near the tulip bed. Bill Barnes, the Barnes's police dog, the terror of the village, was trotting along the sidewalk down on St. Clair. Daddy took out his gold watch. The 6:38 to Detroit would be along in another ten minutes, if it was on time. Across the tracks he could see Al way up in the field getting the cows together to bring them in for their evening milking. In the Fosters' kitchen Helen was cooking dinner, and John came out to water the roses in his back garden.

Daddy went over to join John and the two of them stood there in the drive, Daddy doing most of the talking while John absent-mindedly squirted the hose back and forth.

In our kitchen the pork roast smelled delicious and we were all hot and perspiring. Flies buzzed against the back door screen.

"Vanessa, will you tuck in your shirt. Humor Mama."

"I was going to and I forgot," I said, humiliated. I went into the living room and looked in the mirror. I tucked in my shirt, pulled it down tight to show my bosom. My face looked bumpy. I went upstairs and combed my hair and put on lipstick, a dark purplish color. Then I rubbed it mostly off. I pinched my cheeks and tipped back my head so my eyes were soft slits with lashes and my nose a soft short thing and my wavy hair flowed down my back. That way I thought I was pretty. But I couldn't go around like that. I stuck out my tongue at myself and went downstairs, pinching my cheeks until I reached the kitchen door.

Mama said, "Vanessa, go tell Daddy supper is ready."

Out in the drive I stood and listened. Daddy was telling John about a false Camay put out in Siam, and about his efforts to protect P and G's trademarks there. The hose squirted and I smelled the roses, the wet earth, the new-cut grass. I loved to listen to Daddy talk. When he finished the story, I said, "Supper is ready, Daddy." And we went back toward the house. Daddy put his arm around my waist.

58

"You're a good girl, Vanessa," he said. But I thought he thought I was repulsive. I thought he loved Lisa best.

Just as we reached the back steps we heard the train whistling, coming up the valley. The bells began to ring down at Oak Road. The train whistled coming toward the crossing, and it went by with a great roar, so fast the windows looked like falling dominoes. Then sounds emerged anew and sweet in the evening air—a dog barking, birds singing, the rubber hum of a car going by on St. Clair, Mrs. Hart calling, "Oh, Diana!" I listened to the faint far rumble of the train where it went beyond the village, around the curve, and into the woods, and I thought of distant fields and farms and cities to the north. Daddy took out his watch. "It's running eight and a half minutes behind schedule," he said.

At dinner Mama put her hand on my leg. I hated her to touch my leg.

After supper Lisa and I were out in front. I said, "Lisa, I wish the boys would like me."

"You act too young," Lisa said.

"What do you mean?" I said miserably.

"I don't know. That's what the boys said."

"Who said that?"

"Never mind."

"Tell me who, Lisa."

"I know I'm being mean," she said, "but I'm just paying you back for how mean you were to me before I was five and learned how to protect myself."

"I wasn't ever mean to you."

"Yes you were too."

"I wasn't now, dammit."

"All right for you, Vanessa," she said. "What about the time you said Stevie Jones won the wee-wee contest?"

That was the thing Lisa always harped back to. I never could understand why she took my *decision* so hard. We were down the yard in the patch of soft grass where we liked to play with the hollyhock ladies, and Stevie and Lisa had to wee-wee so I told them to have a contest. They weren't more than three or four and I was two years older. They took off their pants and stood side by side, their plump white legs a little bit apart. Stevie stopped and started while Lisa just went straight from beginning to end. I said Stevie won. Lisa said it wasn't fair because I didn't say how would be the best way to wee-wee. She could have stopped and started two times too. She could have if she'd known. She cried, mortified and furious.

I didn't know why it had upset her so. I didn't understand how *hard* she was trying to beat Stevie Jones and how much power I had in her heart.

"Well, you're the mean one now," I said.

"That's another thing wrong with you, Vanessa," she said. "You're too nice. That's what they say."

I wanted to smack her. My hand felt sick and horrible from feeling how it would feel to hit her flesh, to hurt her.

I went up to my room and shut the door and threw myself down on my bed. I hated myself. I was just a big embarrassed wart who had to hide in the ladies' room at the Cotillion. Then I had to fill in my program in different handwritings so Mama wouldn't know when she asked to see my program. Why did Mama make me feel so ashamed all the time? Once when Owen Hart roughhoused with me in the back seat on the way home from dancing school, I was having so much fun, and Mama said right in front of everyone, "Well, if this is the sort of thing you like, I don't know why I send you to dancing school." I hated Mama. I hated Lisa. Daddy was the only nice one, but he thought I was repulsive. Why did I have to be so ugly? Why did I have to grow so tall?

I tried to read my history assignment. I got a pencil

and underlined. But I couldn't read. I was daydreaming they all died in a car accident. It was so sad I
nearly cried. I had to take care of myself and live
alone. I had an operation to shorten me and another
to make my face pretty. I had lots of clothes—a long,
sliding closet full of clothes—and I built a swimming
pool in our front yard. Owen Hart and all the boys
came over to swim. I imagined I was having trouble
climbing out and Owen Hart pulled me up out of the
water. We were shining with water and silvery in the
moonlight. "Vanessa, I love you," he said. "I love you
too, Owen," I whispered back. Then he kissed me, a
real movie kiss.

Just then Mama called up from downstairs, "Vanessa, it's ten-thirty. You ought to be in bed."

"But, Mama, I haven't finished my homework
yet," I called back.

I went over to the window and pushed up the
screen and climbed out onto the roof and stood there
wanting to fly down among the fireflies and out to
the branch of the maple tree whose huge leaves shiv-
ered in the hot dark night.

I hated myself for having these daydreams and I
couldn't keep from having them. They made me so
I couldn't do my homework. "Now you stop it, Va-

nessa!" I'd say furiously, but then I felt hollow and clamped, the daydreams stopped but I couldn't concentrate anyhow and pretty soon there I'd be again daydreaming of boys.

If only we were in Michigan! If only school were out!

Finally it was. In the terrible heat and the sun, the maple leaves thickened until they were almost black. Ragweed grew up in the cinders along the railroad tracks. Kroupa panted and slobbered all day and drank thirstily from his dog bowl. "Slurp, slurp," Daddy said at dinner. "*Dad*dy," we said lovingly.

We could hardly wait to leave for Neah. We made little piles of what would go, we started saving clothes. "Only eight more days." We said it several times. All over the village shades were pulled down and windows kept shut through the heat of the day. We swam in Grandmother Marston's pool. We put chairs in the pool and sat on them. I wandered through the streets, dizzy and weak from the heat, my shirt soaking wet. I popped the tar bubbles glistening in the sun and squooshed warm tar under my tennis shoe feet, and ended up at Janey's house where we lounged in her cool yellow-darkened living room with its smooth rugless floor. We drank Cokes in tall glasses filled with ice cubes. We decided to have a party and invite the boys and then faint; the boys would be knights and catch us in their arms. We practiced fainting and laughed a lot. Janey laughed really and I laughed trying. Her laughing looked like it felt so good.

"Only two more days," Lisa and I said, and we brought our suitcases down from the attic.

That night we went to Grandpa Nye's for dinner for the last time until September. I walked with Lisa up the walk we used to run up when we were children, and we waited close to the door for Olympia to come and let us in. Grandpa Nye came to the door of the library to greet us. His hands and face were a little moist from the heat.

"Hello, Papa," Daddy said.

Aunt Janice came down from upstairs, her shoes clacking on the stairs which were wide and grand, of shining red cherry wood, with a white spoked bannister that extended all around the upstairs hall. "Hello, dears," she said to Lisa and me, and her voice rose up into her shrill hee hee hee. "Morgan, Isabel," she said, kissing Daddy and Mama.

They went into the library. Lisa and I stayed to pay our respects to Calvin. His nose twinkled on our shins. "Poor Calvin," we said, patting his newly washed coat. "Poor boy," we whispered. "Does your mother wash you in Dreft? Yes!" He wagged his shaggy tail.

Then we drifted around to look at the cats on the velvet shelves of the tall thin cases in the entrance hall. There were beautiful cats and funny cats and grotesque wooden cats from Japan posing in foolish poses. There were cats from China, India, Persia, Egypt, England, Austria, and France.

"No one knows how it began," Daddy told us. "Papa's many wealthy friends began to return from their travels abroad bringing him cats circa 1901–1904. I think Papa thought it would amuse his mother on her round-the-world trips to pick up cats for him, and wherever Papa traveled he picked up cats. They just picked up anything from cat jewelry to holy cows, and cheap replicas to the expensive mummy from Luxor. They picked up jades, brass, woods, rare porcelain, porphyry, bronzes of merit, and marbles, as well as pottery not to be sneezed at."

At each cabinet Lisa and I pressed a switch and little light bulbs lit the shelves from the back so that cat surfaces shone and cats cast miniature shadows. Strands of amber beads wound in and out among them, and we looked at them through fragile glass doors. In a miniature frame with a tiny flag on top was a picture of Uncle Charles and Uncle Edward and Cousin Cato in their uniforms in the First World War—a black cat at their feet for luck. They had it taken in Bordeaux before they went to the front. Here and there was a scarab, or a hunk of rock with mercury, or our uncles' medals from the war, or a piece of fluorspar from one of the mines once owned by the Morgan Burke Company down in Kentucky. But mainly there were cats. There were cats dancing, playing billiards, sketching, climbing up the walls at the backs of the cabinets. Cats were scratching themselves. Cats were bathing themselves. Cats sat with dignity or walked majestically. Way in the back of a low shelf was a dog with a fly on its belly. "Look, Vanessa," Lisa used to say every time she discovered that fly.

At the bottom of the corner hall cabinet was a door that pulled down on its hinges, and inside in the space built especially for it was the tin-can container of the long-interred cat my great-grandmother, Vanessa, purchased in Luxor in 1908. Sometimes, with

Daddy's supervision, we got it out to have a look, but usually, ever since I could remember, the mummy from Egypt was out traveling from school to school in Cincinnati. Once our class in Glendale had an Egyptian exhibit especially so we could have that mummy to ourselves for a while, and then it lay on a shelf in the school hall, a bandaged thing under bright lights.

"When it arrived in Cincinnati in 1908," Daddy said, "Papa had it x-rayed to make certain it was a cat. It was. One of my great pleasures at the time—I was seven then—was to get the smelly thing out and show it around to the guests."

"Lisa and Vanessa," Grundpa Nye said, "did you know that in ancient Egypt when this cat died the inhabitants of the house shaved off their eyebrows?"

Over by the closet under the stairs sat the big wooden cat. It was crudely carved and real—it had a being in it. Very early Lisa and I discovered that if you lifted its head you found Grandpa Nye's wonderful collection of canes inside—polished canes, and crooked canes, and canes with silver knobs. There was a totem cane from Mexico and a white-birch cane that Grandpa Nye picked up on the Albany River in 1923. When we were the same height as the cat, we

67

used to look into its face for magic every time just before we left Grandpa Nye's. When we looked into its face we looked into its eyes, and its eyes were turned into itself. Itself was the canes we knew to be inside.

Once when Grandpa Nye saw me looking at the cat, he asked me if I didn't want one of the canes. I said, "No thank you, Grandpa Nye," but I almost said, "But couldn't I please have one when you die?"—and then I felt horrible. I didn't want him to die, ever.

Now idly I lifted the wooden cat's head and looked down on the canes. I touched a cool silver knob, and then we went into the library, where presently Grandpa Nye said, "Lisa and Vanessa, how would you like to go down to the cellar with me to select the wine for dinner?"

Aunt Janice, who was putting anchovies on crackers, sighed all over them. "Oh, Nate!" she said in her shrill voice. She took an anchovy and squeezed it in two.

We always went. It was the only time we got to have him to ourselves. Since we were children, following along after him close to his suits, which, unlike Daddy's perfect businessman's suits, were always a little rumpled and dusty from his woodpile, his wine cellar, his books, we felt a particular possessive sense of being in connection with our grandfather, who was connected to History.

When we came back to the library Aunt Janice said, "Nate, will you look at your hands now!" In a minute she said, "Go wash them, dear." She giggled like a little girl as he went out of the room. "It's worse than taking care of a small boy," she said with delight.

Olympia appeared at the end of the long dark library to announce dinner, and Daddy grabbed up his martini. He drained it in an angry gulp, and wiped his mouth with his cocktail napkin.

At dinner Grandpa Nye said grace. He poured the wine. Mama smiled and her face absorbed the many colors of the mosaic lampshade that hung down over the table center. Daddy leaned forward and spoke with the special gentleness, the focus, the immaculate attention with which he always spoke to Grandpa Nye. "Papa, what did you think of Henry's paper the other night?" He was talking about a paper at the Literary Club.

Olympia in her black uniform slipped softly

around the table as if she were continually begging pardon. Aunt Janice picked up her fork and leaned forward to talk to Mama. There was a blue tension in her pale skin, her thin lips. She described what the bridesmaids in her niece's wedding wore and how the groom said, "Mrs. Nye, you look so charming in blue." Her eyelids slid, twitching, down over her pupils.

In deep and ruminating voices Grandpa Nye and Daddy talked, ranging back through time. They talked about the old canoe trips. They talked about battles and battlefields. Grandpa Nye had read Parkman and walked the Plains of Abraham, calling forth in his mind the battle there. He had been over all the battlefields of the Revolution and the Civil War, as well as the battlefields at Fallen Timbers, Tippecanoe, and the Thames. He had also stood where Birnam Wood came to Dunsinane.

Grandpa Nye said, "Lisa and Vanessa, when you drive to Neahtawantah the day after tomorrow, you will start off along the course of the original road General Anthony Wayne cut through the forest in 1792 and 3 and 4. As you drive, think of the forest then, and imagine the work of felling trees of great magnitude. Imagine the Indian marauders lurking in the forest and the slow heroic march of General Wayne's men. The names of many of the places you will pass through take their names from that proud campaign. Hamilton was Fort Hamilton. Seven Mile Village was the place where General Wayne's army camped seven miles north of Fort Hamilton. Seven Mile Creek takes its name from the Village . . ."

Grandpa Nye refilled the wine goblets. "Isabel," he said to Mama, "you and I are the only ones in the family with true hollow legs." High up around the molding the plates of all nations were lined up, smiling.

When Uncle Charles and Uncle Edward were there, there were still more stories—about their travels in Spain before the war, about the Great War and after. There was a story I loved about bedbugs in the Balkans, and there were stories about Queen Marie of Rumania when Uncle Charles was there as Chief of Mission administering food after the war—how lovely she was, how gracious, how she could command men with a look in her eye.

After dinner when Lisa and I went up to Aunt Janice's bathroom and shut ourselves in, Lisa said,

"Sometimes I have the urge to hit her. She talks about Grandpa Nye's hands exactly the way she does about Calvin's feet when he's been out in wet weather."

"And forgotten his little red dog galoshes," I said. I giggled.

Aunt Janice's bathroom was soft and alive and secretly filthy with pink rayon pants and slips and silk stockings hanging everywhere so we couldn't help brushing against them. It smelled of talcum powder, and the laundry bag on the back of the door was plump.

"Poor Calvin," Lisa said, sitting on the toilet, giggling.

"Ooox-goox," Lisa said, pointing to the hairs in the bath-tub.

Before going down we walked around the upstairs hall to look at the old pictures and recover our dignity.

We stopped in front of a picture of Daddy when he was three, riding on Uncle Joab's shoulders. Daddy had long curls and he was grinning. He was holding onto Uncle Joab's forehead. It was taken the famous day that Grandpa Nye said, "Now, boys, today I'm going to illustrate the *eee*vils of gambling." He took them over the river to Kentucky, put a nickel in a slot machine in the first place they entered, said, "Boys, the *eee*vils of gambling are being illustrated," and out came an enormous bucketful of coins. "It was like that all day," Daddy said. "Papa couldn't lose." When Daddy got tired, Uncle Joab carried him on his shoulders and let him look in the windows of all the evil places they didn't enter.

Grandmother Nye used to make Daddy dress up like Little Lord Fauntleroy, and he hated that. She wanted his curls long too, and when Daddy was five Uncle Charles took him downtown to the barbershop and had his hair cut. When they got home Grandmother Nye turned red with fury. She tried to get Grandpa Nye to beat Uncle Charles.

We stopped in front of a picture of Mama and Daddy paddling a canoe on a lake in Canada when they were fifteen.

"Look, Vanessa," Lisa said, "they have on their Smelly-Boys!"

Grandpa Nye got the Smelly-Boys (canvas hunting jackets so named because of how they smelled when they were dry-cleaned) at Abercrombie & Fitch in the spring of 1916. "Papa ordered a dozen at once, as I recall," Daddy said.

Now Lisa and I had taken over Mama's and Daddy's Smelly-Boys. They no longer smelled. We kept them at Neah and walked through the woods in them and felt alike and good with jackets like soft worn tents around us. "I can't wait," I said, thinking of how it would feel to breathe the cool air of the woods.

"Me either," said Lisa.

We stopped in front of the enormous picture of Alfred, Grandpa Nye's Indian guide, standing on the rocks, holding a pair of deer antlers. "I wish we could have known Alfred," I said.

In *Summer Wanderings in Northern Canada* Grandpa Nye wrote, "I did not know when I met Alfred McCloud, my Indian guide, at Sans Souci in 1897 that we were to continue our association for many years and that a warm and enduring friendship was to blossom in our lives, but that was what happened. Alfred was a man of feeling, of high character, and with an appreciation of Nature that was unusual in an Indian. I verily believe that his delight in the beauty of the land and water was as great as mine. He had a great fund of knowledge of the ways of fishes and beasts, and was full of the traditions of the Indians, and was able to hold his own in conversation. He had been graduated from the Indian Normal School at Brantford, had taught in the Indian schools at

74

Curve Lake and on the Christian Islands. He was, in fact, not only a superior Indian, but a superior man. He was as tall as I and he was handsome. He was expert in handling a canoe even in the most dangerous waters and he knew the northland, its rivers and lakes."

"In winter," Daddy said, "when Alfred came to visit us, he liked to go down to the Queen City Club each morning—dressed in Nathaniel J. Nye's clothes of course—and install himself in the library where he read and smoked expensive cigars."

"He was not a wild Indian," Uncle Edward told me once when I asked him. "He was a gentleman and a scholar. When he came to visit Papa, he was written up in all the papers."

Years after this time I found among Grandpa Nye's letters at the Cincinnati Historical Society a letter from Alfred written in May, 1925, from the Chemong Reserve, and then I knew Alfred as I had not from what I had heard, for then I knew the power of his eloquence and the bitter sorrow for his people that he bore in his heart. He wrote, "I did not go back to Mississaiga District last fall to hunt as I purposed. I heard the places were all located by the hunters, of course white men. A white man who is comfortably housed and have plenty to eat and wear and can afford to stay home and be served luxuries, for mear having a nice time he goes camping and catching the little animals which once afford sustenance to the poor Indian. Once the lordly Indian held sway and had sole control of these hunting grounds, but today the white man hold supremacy, and the poor Indian has to stand back and come back to the reserve and hunt what few animals may have sought refuge from the deadly weapons of the white man. Today in Ontario there are ten white men hunting to one Indian. You must understand I mean the residents of Ontario— Farmers, Merchants, etc. These are the culprits whose ambition (unknowingly) is to deprive the Indians of their birth right. I regret I can not furnish you with any items from hunting as you requested for your lecture with only the few muskrats I caught on the shores of the Chemong Reserve."

Alfred had a brushy white mustache, dark skin with a metallic smoothness, and dreamy, gentle eyes. He had a long hooked nose like Daddy's and Grandpa Nye's. When we got back to the library, I said, "Grandpa Nye, did anyone ever think you and Alfred looked like each other?"

Grandpa Nye smiled, his eyes glinted at me.

76

"Hiro!" he said in a stentorian voice. "'Hiro' means 'I have spoken.' It was the term with which the Iroquois used to end all their speeches and was the origin of the French name for the Indian tribes of the Long House, the Five Nations, later Six, the Iroquois."

"Hiro," I repeated, learning, my face flushed with excitement.

"Alfred, of course, was Ojibway," Grandpa Nye said, "and the Iroquois were formerly their deadly enemy.

"Did I ever tell you about your father's introduction to the Canadian wilds?"

"No," we said.

"He was fourteen months old," Grandpa Nye said. "Alfred used to go to Pointe au Baril a week before our arrival, bringing other guides to prepare our camp for us. The year after Morgan was born we came by steamer from Penetang and arrived at the Point at six in the morning. It was a raw, foggy morning. Alfred was on the wharf, waiting. After the usual greetings Alfred calmly took Morgan from Antoinette, his nurse, and asked Mrs. Nye his name.

"Thereupon without another word he had one of the other Indians load up his canoe and into the lading he tucked Morgan. He paddled off without saying anything more. Antoinette was almost in hysterics. The idea of an Indian disappearing in the fog with the baby, and in a frail canoe at that, was too much for her. But when we arrived at Rattlesnake Island, we found Morgan safe and sound, playing with a snake. Non-poisonous. Alfred had a fire going, and speedily we had breakfast prepared. Morgan had his first flapjack."

Daddy grinned and then, as he always did at 9:20 when he went to Grandpa Nye's for dinner, he put his hand in his vest pocket and pulled out his watch, and said, "Well, it is now 9:20."

We all got up. In the hall Aunt Janice caught hold of Daddy's arm and clung to it. "Those *stairs*, Morgan! Nate is going to fall on those *stairs*," she said, her voice wailing "*stairs*."

Grandpa Nye was standing by the library door with the detached dignity he assumed when Aunt Janice discussed his person. I went over to him to say good night. He took my arm as if he were going to tell me something, and then he dropped it. I kissed him. "Good night, good night," he said as if he had already said good night and retired.

"Good night, dear." Aunt Janice kissed me.

"Good night, poor Calvin," I whispered.

I carried a bottle of Grandpa Nye's wine for Daddy, and when we reached the lamp at the street I held it up to look at the cylindrical well of light in the white wine. Just then Aunt Janice turned the light out from its switch in the front hall, and we were left in the dark. Daddy was fiddling with the car keys. "Damn," he said. Then he got the car door open. "Come on, Vanessa," Mama said.

It was almost 3:30 in the morning the day of the trip. I got up and went to the window. Still black night. The trees were leafy masses not stirring in the hot humid air. Then high up out at the edge of the yard the ash trees whispered.

The alarm went off in Mama and Daddy's room. I knew how they were lying side by side in their bed in the dark. Their cigarettes glowed red in front of their faces, faded to the side, flared up again when they took a puff, and flew finally into the darkness of an ash tray on either side of the bed.

The toilet flushed. I went down the hall to Lisa's

room. Mama came to open their door and Kroupa dashed out to greet us. He licked my face. "Kroupa!" I said. "Pugh!" Mama had on her nightgown we could see through. I thought it was disgusting. Her eyes were puffy and her hair a bit strandy and wild. "Shh, now children, don't wake the Fosters," Mama whispered.

"Daddy," I whispered, running into their room. "Kroupa's halitosis is worse than ever. What will we do?"

"I suggest a thorough purge," Daddy said, a little hoarse, standing by the bureau in his pajamas, his dark hair rumpled and soft, his eyes without glasses—just the deep red mark they made across the bridge of his long hooked nose.

After we backed out of the garage Daddy said in his deep matter-of-fact voice, "The time is exactly 4:35 Eastern Standard Time, and the mileage is 4735.8."

While he closed the garage door, Lisa and I noted these facts in our notebooks, feeling happy and excited about how we were settled into our places in the gentle darkness of the car.

"Good-bye, house," we called, looking back at it, sleeping and gray, the windows cool eyes.

80

The village square was empty and dark except for the harsh white light in Igler's Drugstore window.

When we turned out onto the highway and started going fast, the car filled with a whirring roar. The headlights faded grayer on the road. In Hamilton we stopped for a red light and nothing passed as we waited.

"Seven Mile Creek," Lisa said when we went over it the first time.

To the east the sky reddened and Mama said dreamily, "Red sky in the morning, sailors take warning."

In the early light we whizzed by fields of wheat and corn and clover, by wood patches and farmhouses and barns.

I said, "Leave Preble County, Enter Darke County."

As we entered Greenville, Daddy said pontifically, "Here in 1795, following the victory of General Anthony Wayne over the Indians at Fallen Timbers, was signed the Treaty of Greenville, whereby the Indians relinquished the land to the south and east, and the immense Northwest Territory was opened to settlement."

We drove up a cobblestone street and around the

huge ugly old brick courthouse right in the center of the street. I imagined the Indians and General Wayne with his men climbing the steps of the courthouse to sign the Treaty, and then I remembered this was all forest then and Greenville was a wooden fort.

At seven we stopped for gas in Fort Wayne. The sun was already high and the day was a hot one. Outside of town the car slowed and Mama poured Daddy a drink. The fresh smell of gin filled the car.

"Hark, a park!" Daddy said, as we passed one. We all laughed.

We recalled our first trip to Neah. How horrible it was! We were in the old blue Plymouth and Daddy had his carbuncle in the middle of his forehead. There was terrible summer heat, silver sunlight. It was the drought. I still could see Daddy's soft white bandage on his forehead and smell the hydrosol and feel his acute discomfort which was like an animal running under his skin; but we were in the back seat with Sandy, our puppy, and Helen, our maid for the summer. She had purple spots on her fat white arms and I didn't like being squeezed in so close to her. Then we were sitting on the back seat by a ditch in Indiana because we had a flat tire, and Daddy had to get the tools out from under the back seat. It was 1932, and Daddy didn't have a job. Mama said, "Children, the Girl of the Limberlost lived near here."

Now Daddy said, "It was just along here, Isabel."

Mama said, "Children, it's wonderful now you're getting old enough for us to enjoy you."

We drove fast through fields of high corn. I got out my notebook and wrote: "7:30, June 27, 1941. North of Fort Wayne. Fields of corn where in former days the Indians too had vast fields of corn. Think!—the crop is the same as when the Indian tilled the soft black earth with a crooked stick and cultivated the growing corn with a clam shell hoe . . ."

On another page I started writing, "Oh think of Tecumseh, bold and daring, think of Tecumseh tall and strong, think of his warriors, four hundred warriors in full war paint coming down the Wabash through the forest . . ."

Lisa leaned over and tried to see what I was writing. I grabbed my notebook to me. She spoiled my mood and I squnched around miserably.

"Move over, Vanessa. You're on my side," she said nastily.

I sat up stiff and rolled down the window. I wanted

to be out of the car. I wanted to be in Neah swimming, sailing, sailing the *Annabel Lee* with Dirk Monroe.

"Vanessa, roll up your window, please," Daddy said, irritated.

I shut it, humiliated. Why did I do everything wrong?

It got hotter. Kroupa began to pant and slobber. "Get down Kroupa," I said. "Stay down."

Lisa and I decided to play the animal game, but pretty soon we quarreled. "There were *not* twenty cows in that field, Vanessa."

"There were too, I counted them," I said.

"Count the legs and divide by four is the only foolproof system," Daddy said.

All day Mama's and Daddy's voices blended into the whir of the car and emerged again talking when we slowed down to go through a town.

In the afternoon south of Cadillac the land changed and the white road stretched from long fir-covered hill to hill. Mama said as she did every year that this was certainly the most beautiful road in the country, this stretch of Michigan 115.

About three o'clock we stopped for groceries at

Krogers in Traverse City, and then we drove the twelve miles on out to Neahtawantah on the low road that wound along by West Bay.

When we were going by the Island I saw the *Annabel Lee*. "Look, Lisa, there they are. There are Dirk and Elihu. See them!" I pointed, and as I did the white sails grayed like the wings of a gull changing direction high in the sunlit air, the sails vanished and emerged again, white, way out there in the blue water distance. "They came about!"

The cottage in the shade of the beech trees looked small. The kitchen wall was splattered with sandy raindrops and there were cobwebs in the woodpile. When I got out of the car my knees felt flimsy. The air was cool and smelled of the damp forest floor.

Inside was the musty odor of winter and wood walls. I touched the canvas arm of my Smelly-Boy hanging on its hook at the foot of the stairs. My stone and sand were still in its pocket.

Then I went back for more suitcases. Daddy was leaning against the beech tree by the woodpile. He looked very pale and tired. "Kroupa's full of beans," he said.

On hot afternoons I lay on my cot on the sleeping porch reading, and I remembered in my body afternoons when we were little when we took our naps on our cots in the green afternoon heat that came in through the beech leaves and knew without knowing that Mama and Daddy lay naked together in their sun-hot room with a silver white fire blending their white bodies. It made us restless and apprehensive and sensual too, next to our sheets, close to the forest.

I got up, enchanted in my book, and walked, carrying it, through the woods. My throat was burning. My body was dreaming of love. I went up the beach to Boys' Hut and took off my clothes and lay on the sand and put my lips in the water. And the sun, the golden red black heat of the sun warmed me, drugged me, all the long afternoon; and the water took me in its sweet green depths, in its moving waves, in the rhythm of its waves falling and withdrawing with bubbles on the sand. I lay reading in the sand in the heat and felt the west wind blowing softly and felt the blue green bay blowing, frothing, falling white gently in the sunlight.

Later I went into the forest. I went to the place where the virgin maples were and got out my mirror and looked at myself in the green forest light. I saw the pale maple leaves high above and I thought my skin was green the way Rima's in *Green Mansions* was. I dreamed that some day I would come here to the virgin maple grove and Dirk would be here leaning against a tall tree trunk and he would be different. We would be strangers and beautiful the way we had been one night in the woods coming back from West Bay when our hands touched accidentally in the dark and I felt a deep shock of sensation. Another night after that we all built a fire on the beach near Fisherman's Hut, and his hand touched mine under the sand. We sat there a long time touching hands deep in the grainy sand. We twined and rubbed our fingers against each other's. We pretended we didn't know.

In the evening Lisa and I went down to the Monroes', but after we got there we couldn't decide what to do so we just messed around on their front porch. It was hot. Below was Bower's Harbor, glassy calm with evening clouds and the hills of the far shore reflected. The *Annabel Lee* stood straight, pointing at her mooring, her tall mast mirrored too. I imagined the sweet sounds of the water against her and I wished that we were out in a canoe. Lisa and Elihu were reading a comic together on the swing, and

Dirk was teasing me. "Oh, Vanessa," Dirk said as if he knew something secret and embarrassing about me.

The blood was racing in my head. I was all wild nerve ends. "Oh, Vanessa," Dirk said again, standing there smiling in his white tee-shirt, his arms and chest strong and muscular. "Dirk, stop it!" I said, angrily stamping my foot and then laughing excitedly. He was grinning, pleased. His face had a nice rough look with his pimples sunburned and with the nice rough look of shaving. He had a wet, very red mouth and high cheekbones and a very high forehead and sunburned blond hair with a cowlick sticking up. "Oh, Vanessa," he repeated, shaking his head and looking suddenly serious. "Dirk!" I said. I wanted to touch him but I hit him. I was only playing, I didn't mean to hit him, but I hit him again.

Then I saw that he . . . I saw through his blue pants that I'd made him . . . I just sort of turned and walked casually away as if I hadn't seen, and when I got out on the sidewalk I started to run. How could we look at anyone again? Poor him. It was my fault because I hit him and that made him stick out that way so big under his pants. I felt miserable. How could we ever look at each other?

88

But we did. He took me sailing and he taught me how to sail. We were released, sailing out across the harbor, the water deep beneath us, the green keel sliding through it, bubbles boiling in the wake, waves splashing on the bow, the soft sails stiff and full. The wind—I loved the wind. I held the tiller and felt its pull. Sometimes out in West Bay I lay out on the bow so the waves would splash on my face, my hair, my whole body, and then I'd go back, shining and soaking wet and sit beside Dirk, our bare legs braced side by side across the cockpit.

At night Lisa and Elihu had to go in at ten o'clock, but Dirk and I got to stay out until ten-thirty. Dirk's grandmother was teaching us to play bridge. Over on the piano was the picture of Dirk's Uncle Dirk who was killed in France in 1918. He was pale and blond, his hair was parted in the center, and he had a very smooth, handsome face. At ten-thirty Dirk's grandmother said, "Now, Dirk, you walk Vanessa home."

"Aw, Granny, do I have to?" Dirk would say.

"Yes, Dirk, you do," she said.

As we walked along past the cottages, we looked in the windows. At the Bowdens' we saw Aunt Aggie sitting on Uncle Harry's lap and they were laughing and happy. We walked along by the Old Hotel Grounds, heard the flickering aspen leaves, and the sumac, and we stepped on the cement block where, years ago before the fire, the guests alit from their carriages.

Dirk picked a piece of high grass and he sucked it. The Big Dipper hung low over the dark line of woods beyond the field we crossed. We went between the junipers into the Indian path we made when we were little and had our tepee. It was as if we had no connection with those children who used to play Truth or Consequences in the tepee and show each other their wee-wee places for Consequences, and sometimes get to touch them too. (Dirk and Elihu showed us how they could make theirs go up so they could carry their towels to West Bay on them, all the way through the woods if no one came along to see.)

Now we were mysterious. We weren't bad any more. We weren't used to each other at all. We were in some way as strange and shy as when we first saw each other the first year our family came to Neah. I was five and a half and I was invited to Dirk Monroe's birthday party. He was seven. He was standing in the sunlight across the green lawn near the little birch-log cabin. There were children dressed in party clothes playing on the lawn between the grapevine wall on one side and the long flower garden on the other. Beyond were tall trees. Dirk was wearing white shorts and a white shirt and his blond hair was shining in the sun and was full of light, and his skin was blond and soft. I wanted to be next to him.

He didn't notice me, but he stayed in my mind that way like a dream through summer, and winters, and in my mind I imagined I walked across the lawn and through the children playing and up to Dirk, all warm from the sun, and our faces touched and he put his arms around me and we went away to a place in the shade where there was a bed of violets and there we sat down and he kissed me and our skins touched and we blended into each other.

Now we came out of the path and crossed the sand and roots road to our cottage. I said, "Well, good night. Thanks for walking me home." I was standing close to him.

"Yeah, good night," he said, not looking at me.

I went up the stairs and into the cottage and threw myself down on the couch in despair. Why didn't he want to kiss me? Lisa had been kissed lots of times. She'd even gone steady and had a pretend engagement ring and she was only thirteen. What was *wrong* with me?

I went into the bathroom and looked into the mirror. I really had gotten prettier, hadn't I? I used to be sallow, completely ugly, but now (since the coming of the dark blood) there was rosiness in my cheeks. There was glow in my sun-browned skin, and my hair was softer, nicer. Wasn't it? But my hickies. It was my hickies that made me repulsive. I pinched one. I squeezed. I hated myself.

Why couldn't I be right in front of people? Why couldn't I talk right? Sometimes I felt so tense and ashamed in front of people I thought I might scream and go crazy. The only thing to do was go away, and run through the woods to the beach and try to get rid of my horrible self, my ugly face, my tall, awkward body. I ran up the beach to the point where I could see the long wooded arms of the bay stretching north and far out between them the Open Lake, and then with the wide clean band of Lake Michigan in my mind, I walked lightly, I ran, my arms stretched out like the wings of a bird. When I got tired enough and hot, I'd take off my clothes and go into the water and swim under water looking into the smooth greeny distance.

Other days, when the wind was gray and the air was soft, a secret mood was stirred inside me and I went off exultant through the forest which was blowing so it sounded like waves breaking on a distant shore, and I walked on the beach in a state of ecstasy, saying the lines of my poems with the voices in the wind.

> Grey sky and wind and water softly blow
> Wave on wave, stirring silken depths beneath,
> Stirring in my mind a flow
> Of words urging Not only feel the water,
> Not only feel but *be* the water.
> Dissolve! Return!

On a dark Saturday late in October the year before, I had had a violent experience—a vision, or a revelation, or the appearance of a ghost, I don't know what to call it, but I would never forget it. I was alone in our house in the study, old books around me. I had been reading *Beowulf* and I had begun to write a long poem about the dam of Grendel, the misty mere, a dark cave. My mind was drugged with the fire and darkness of my vision. Night was coming on at the windows. I was walking back and forth in a trance, half out of myself, when, for some reason, I pulled *The Nye Family Record* out from the shelf, opened it idly at a point in the middle and read what Grandpa Nye wrote:

"My maternal grandfather, the Reverend Hezekiah Gordon DeGolyer, died the summer before I was born. All that I know about him is hearsay. He, too, like my Grandfather Nye, was a Baptist minister. . . .

"This Grandfather DeGolyer was a different kind of man from Grandfather Nye. He was more volatile; he had a great love of out-door life and was a hunter and a fisher. In the summer of 1862 he was with a party of friends on the Great Lakes. As their little boat was passing through the Straits of Mackinac a sudden squall tore the jib boom loose. It swung around and knocked my grandfather overboard. In that way he lost his life. Some time later two bodies were washed ashore on a broad beach on Northern Lake Michigan. The fishermen buried them where they were found. Members of the family went to the place with the hope of being able to identify and bring back my grandfather's body. But, while they thought it highly probable that one of the bodies washed ashore was his, they could not be sure."

For a moment he was there behind me in the room—my great-great-grandfather whose face I did not know. I felt him there, I saw him—but not with my eyes. And after a minute it was as if somehow I were him, and yet as if I remembered him. I tried turning mentally to remember, but I could see only his dark hair, his hairline, his forehead—like Daddy's forehead long ago. The rest blurred white, white body whose presence I had felt as close as if he had come into my mind in a dream I had and now recalled.

It was as if once long ago in the night I had seen him in a carriage in the darkness driving swiftly by. The horses galloped, the curtain dropped, and he was gone; but in that moment I was also in the carriage. I was him. It was my arm which let the curtain drop and I was dead. I had been hit by the boom, and I had seen him sinking down through the blue water darkness of the Straits of Mackinac, down beyond the last rays of light to where he lay in the blue water darkness of the lake floor entwined in long strands of seaweed, his face, his body, his arms, white like phosphorus.

95

After that when I asked Grandpa Nye about his Grandfather DeGolyer, he said, "It saddens me that I know so little about him. He died the summer before I was born, you know. He was but forty-nine and the future was before him. My mother told me I bore him a strong resemblance." In a minute he added, "The DeGolyers dreamed dreams and saw visions."

Now on a gray day when the wind was soft and sweet, as I walked far up the beach where the reeds were beyond Boys' Hut and Fisherman's Hut, my mind dreamed idly off and suddenly (returning) it seemed to me my arm was the arm of my Great-Great-Grandfather DeGolyer. It was my canvas sleeve around my arm, my hand, but the sensation was that it was his. I threw myself down on the sand and the waters of the bay became my mind and my mind stretched to become Lake Michigan, stretched north to the Straits of Mackinac where he was deep down and wrapped in darkness, dead.

Later in July Lisa's friend, Jenny, and my friend, Janey, came to visit, and then we went once a week for a picnic lunch at Boys' Hut. Mama said, "Mad dogs and Englishmen lie out in the noonday sun." Off we went, our picnic baskets heavy with our towels, mirrors, cold creams, sun oils, shampoo, combs, brushes, barrettes, bobby pins, lipsticks, and our razors. We washed and shaved our legs sitting in the stones at the water's edge, and then we swam and shampooed our hair. We rinsed our hair swimming naked in the green under water, our hair flowing, our bodies pale; we swam with our legs together and rubbed against the rippled sand on the lake floor like mermaids. All day we frolicked in the water and baked our bodies in the sun—darker, redder, hotter, so our breasts inside our bathing suits became whiter and more secret and more beautiful. We combed our hair and put on lipstick and looked at ourselves in the mirror to see our eyes bluer in the light of the bay. When we took off our bathing suits to swim we were ashamed until we were in under water. I hid myself where my hair was. "Timberrr!" we called it.

About five o'clock we went home. Upstairs in the cottage it smelled of warm wood. Mama and Daddy were talking harmoniously the way they did when they dressed together before dinner. We could smell witch hazel and gin. When they went by our door on the way downstairs, we could smell Mama's perfume.

The blood beat throbbing in our sunburned skin. We strained to see how burned our backs were in the mirror. "Look at me," said Lisa, "Look at *me*!" said Jenny. We put on clean white bras, clean white underpants, clean white shirts, and our blue jeans which we belted tight. Then we put our arms alongside each other to see who was brownest. "Lisa! Lisa's always the brownest."

Someone backfired. "Oh, pugh! Was that you, Jenny?" Lisa said.

"Light a match," said Janey.

"Help! Someone light a match," I said.

We combed our hair and looked at ourselves profile. We snuck into Mama and Daddy's room to clean our fingernails with Daddy's nail file and look at ourselves in Mama's mirror. We put witch hazel on our mosquito bites.

Downstairs in the kitchen Mama hugged Daddy, which made him look very tall and skinny and embarrassed. "We're living high on the hog tonight," Mama said, smiling and pretty. We were having roast leg of lamb with mint sauce and riced potatoes the way Green, Grandmother Marston's chauffeur, used to make them.

At dinner Daddy said, looking down the table at

her, "Your mother is the world's living beautiful woman."

Another night at dinner Daddy said, "Just pass me a little dash of time and space."

"Do you propose to salt the fourth dimension?" I asked, passing him the salt and pepper. Daddy liked that.

"The Garden of Eden was most probably in Afghanistan," Daddy said. "My brother Joab wanted to go on an expedition to find it."

"Eat your dinner, Morgan," Mama said.

A sudden blurred look came into his eyes and he stared at her.

After a while he said, angrily, positively, "I believe in absolute honesty."

Mama said, "Vanessa, will you *please* stop clutching your milk like that. And sit up straight, dear."

We did the dishes and then we played baseball out in the field until dark. Dirk Monroe came up to bat. "Timberrrr!" Lisa cried as his home run hit went sailing up and out toward the woodpile. Jenny and Janey and I all giggled. Dirk raced intently from base to base.

Sometimes after dark Daddy taught us how to shoot crap with the big dice on our screen porch.

99

He rolled the dice up against the wall. "Come on, seven." "Snake eyes." "Little fever." "Come on, seven." We were all stooped down. My arm was against Dirk's for a moment, and the feel of his skin, his arm, made strange soft fire go all through me. Why didn't he notice me? "Come on, seven," he said, very loud. "Little Joe from Kokomo," Daddy said. He rolled again. "Boxcars," he said. "Come on, seven," said Dirk. Outside high up the leafy forest blew, sounding like a waterfall.

Mama was reading a detective story in the living room, and then she came out on the porch and stood over us. "Your sweater is on inside out, Vanessa." She sighed heavily and picked at my arm. "Go *look* at yourself, dear," she said, sighing again. I went away into the bathroom, burning with shame.

Daddy was funny. He swallowed a minnow from Miss Ellie's bait trap down at Big Dock at two o'clock in the afternoon. He used to swallow goldfish at cocktail parties in the twenties, Mama said. All the Nyes did. One time Cousin Cato swallowed a goldfish worth five hundred dollars. "Imagine his embarrassment," Mama said. Daddy recalled the seal Jim Sutton bought to put in the fountain at the Waldorf to get even with the management. And once at a cocktail party at Princeton he accidentally saw Zelda Fitzgerald passed out naked in the bathtub.

Uncle Harry liked to tell us, "Ladies, did I tell you?" "No," we'd say, happy. And he'd tell us about the famous Fourth of July when they had the mint julep party over in the pavilion at West Bay starting at high noon. He looked up as evening was coming on and there was Mama sitting up in the pine tree drinking mint juleps with Mr. Black.

I imagined it must have been that same famous Fourth of July much later in the graying light when Mr. Murdock went to the bathroom on Mr. Monroe's white flannel pants. "Oh, pardon me, I thought you were a birch tree," Mr. Murdock said.

Jenny and Janey went home and one night after that when the sun had been hot all day on the sandy roads, hot on the glassy bay, Lisa and I went running out into the garden in front of the cottage after supper with the jar of Seeds Mama took for her constipation.

"Mama," we called, "come see us planting the flowering bowels."

All Lisa had to do the whole rest of the summer

was look at me and say, "Vanessa, flowering b . . ." and her eyes would get bluer, melting, and her face would get red, the blood vessels stiffening up under the skin of her forehead, and off we'd go into long glorious fits of laughter. Mama would say sourly, "Their *minds* are in the bathroom again."

That night Mama came out on the porch and said, "Children, take them back upstairs at once."

We did, nearly dropping them ten times from helplessness.

"Seeeeeeeeds, Vanessa," Lisa said, and trying not to, we burst into a fresh uproar of merriment, dissolving on the stairs. "Hold them, Lisa, I can't," I said, passing her the jar. "Seeeeeeeeds, Lisa, oh what will we dooooooooo?"

Later, recovered, and happy together, we decided to go for a night dip in West Bay. It was still hot. We got our towels and our Smelly-Boys to keep the mosquitoes off our arms, and when we came out on the screen porch where Mama and Daddy and Aunt Aggie and Uncle Harry sat drinking highballs, Uncle Harry said, shaking his head, his blue eyes smiling in his handsome red face, "Ladies, you look so much like your mother the first summer she wore the Smelly-Boy."

102

"Oh, do we really?" we said, pleased, and we sat down together on the swing and creaked it back and forth.

"Let's see," Daddy said. "That would have been the summer of 1916. It was your mother's first canoe trip."

"We were fifteen. We thought we were engaged," Mama said, laughing gently.

"The summer of 1916," Daddy said, and he began to recall. "That was the summer of the great portage over the watershed into Lake St. Joseph. We went by way of Lac Seul and Lake St. Joseph to the headwaters of the Albany, then down the Albany to Fort Hope. We returned by Summit Lake, which was right on the Great Divide, to Umbabika. Remember, Isabel, how Dr. Fenway used to come forth in his ponderous voice to place all things in geological time and place."

"Oh, do Uncle Ben, Morgan," Mama said.

Daddy stood up and, opening his mouth to cavernous proportions, he did Uncle Ben the morning he rose at five and paraded back and forth on the rocks in front of the tents bellowing loud enough to rouse, "'I dreamt that I dwelt in marble halls.'"

"Uncle Ben had a sense of humor," Daddy said.

"He was always trying to 'put one over' on Papa. Those two brothers were as different as night and day." Then he did Uncle Ben saying, "Is not God upon the water the same as on the land?"

"I wish you could have seen us," Aunt Aggie shouted in her marvelous voice, "coming into the lobby of the Blackstone after nine weeks in the wilderness."

In *Summer Wanderings in Northern Canada* Grandpa Nye wrote, "Our first canoe trips were in the little lakes north of the Kawarthas, but I longed for something wilder. When the Canadian National Railroad was completed from Cochrane to Winnipeg, it made it possible to reach the very heart of the Canadian Wilderness, and then summer after summer I spent in that marvelous land. The first summer I went down the Shekak and back by the Nagogimi. I think I was never more supremely happy. I could not express myself in prose but turned to verse—not poetry in the great sense but true inspirations, born of the woods and the waters and the uplifting of my soul by the spirit of the wilderness."

After supper in camp, Grandpa Nye used to spread out his arms and say, " 'For God's sake, let us sit upon

104

the ground and tell sad stories of the death of kings.'"

And then he read to them from Shakespeare or the Old Testament.

In *Cedar and Spruce* Grandpa Nye wrote that at night on lonely lakes, as the forest shadows deepened, they heard the loon call, and gathered closer round the fire to recount the day's adventures, while the Indian guides sat silent, lost in dream, their grave impassive faces lighted by the flames, and he wondered did their thoughts run backward, backward to the time before we came.

"We slept on beds of balsam boughs," Mama said dreamily.

"It would be raining cats and dogs," Aunt Aggie shouted. "And Mr. Nye would say, 'It's nothing but a fine Scotch mist.'"

"We had to break camp and press on," Daddy said. "Papa and Alfred paddling out ahead as usual."

"Mr. Nye's flapjacks were delicious," Uncle Harry said.

Then Mama and Daddy, both talking at once, told the story of the moose meat that got too old.

Mama and Dow, her guide, were carrying the

moose meat in their canoe. "It was so high it was as-phyxiating," Mama said. "But Mr. Nye *would not* let us throw it away." Grandpa Nye's rule was that they kill only to eat. Therefore they must eat what they killed.

"Dow was the Irish Indian with a sense of humor," Daddy said. "He was named after Neal Dow, the great temperance man. And Dow managed to just *loooze* that moose meat very neatly one morning when Papa and Alfred disappeared around a bend in the Albany."

Daddy got a piece of paper and made a picture of the canoes. There were ten that summer with, as usual, an Indian guide at the stern of each canoe. He showed all the canoes going along in a line and then one, Mama and Dow's, veering off to the side for the losing of the moose meat.

"We caught fish aplenty," Grandpa Nye wrote in *Summer Wanderings in Northern Canada*. "We hunted the yellow deer and the moose, and we ate blueberries side by side with the black bear, so to speak . . .

"All were canoe trips of the first magnitude, but the most strenuous was when Ben and Charles and Alfred and I descended the Ogoki River. That was difficult and dangerous. It is the wildest river of my experience, full of fierce rapids and glorious water-falls. We came out at the Ogoki Post on the Albany, then we went down the Albany to the English and so to the railroad by way of the Pagwa. It was late August when we reached the Pagwa and it was low. In places the river was a mile wide and six inches deep. For long stretches it flows over smooth water-worn limestone. The water was not deep enough to paddle—we simply had to wade and pull the canoes. I shall always remember the ascent of the Pagwa with horror. In addition to the heavy labor, the weather was bad—a cold drizzle. So we were wet most of the time. That rather took the starch out of us, and when at last we saw Pagwa with the friendly Revillon Post and knew the next day we should have our meals in a dining car and be whisked along in a Pullman, we were overjoyed.

"The greatest in point of distance and interest of all my canoe trips was that in the summer of 1928 to York Factory on Hudson Bay. We went by steamer to the northeast end of Lake Winnipeg where the Nelson River has its birth as a wide expanse of island-studded water. There is situated Norway House, an old impressive Hudson Bay Post, and there we put our canoes in the water, going down the Nelson, thence through a chain of little rivers and lakes to Oxford House at the east end of Oxford Lake, thence to Knee Lake where we came to the headwaters of the Hayes which brought us to York Factory. I shall never forget the moment when at last we saw Hudson Bay and smelled the salt air. We saw low grassy islands way out to sea. We saw whales swimming by, and with a great sweep of the tide we were carried around to the dock at York Factory.

"We had made our way through the unbroken forest, through country unchanged since the days of Christopher Columbus, to a point reached by few white men. At the post at York Factory there were five whites and about 300 Indians. We returned by way of the Nelson, camping a night in its estuary on the finest beach I have ever seen. There were immense boulders and we had to clear the ground of whalebones to make camp because the Indians came to that place in the fall to hunt whales for dog food. The Nelson is a tremendous clear green river flowing with a force like the smooth rush of water before a waterfall, the current 'too deep for sound or foam.' It was impossible to ascend it paddling; we had to ascend it by tracking (towing) until we came to the point where the Limestone falls into it. There we came to the then End of Steel of the Hudson Bay Railroad, which carried us to Le Pas."

"Well, be off, my darling daughters," Mama said. "It's getting late."

Off we went across the field and into the graying woods, our towels around our necks, our hands deep in our canvas pockets. I rubbed my stone I kept there. We walked with the long strides Daddy taught us. We loved the sameness of our legs, our rhythm, our strength. We were sisters! We felt alike, silky skinned and sunburned and lithe inside the soft worn canvas which like another self around us made us *Nyes*, made us feel as we walked through the darkening woods the aura of the greatness of those old days when they went through the wilderness by canoe as the Indians had before them.

"Nye," I said to Lisa.

"Yeah, Nye?" she said.

I remembered once Grandpa Nye said, "When I was a boy I was something like the wild buffaloes of the prairie who would go any distance for water. I would go any distance for a swim. My brother Ben was cut from the same piece of cloth."

"I love it when someone thinks I'm you," I said.

"Oh, I love it when someone thinks I'm you," she said. "Vanessa, remember the time we got hysterics just thinking of the word 'mule.'"

"Yes," I said. "*Mule.*" We giggled a bit.

"And Dirk Monroe's smelly socks!" I said.

"Oh, pugh!" Lisa said.

We smelled the pines near the beach and came out on the quiet water. Far off across the bay the opposite shore was already black. "Bahooom," we called out across the water. We took off our shoes and waded, and up the beach we ran in the gray light in the place where our feet sang rubbing the sand still warm from the sun. Around the point in the cove near Boys' Hut we took off our clothes. The night air was sweet on our skin. We swam, our bodies moon white in the silky night water. Afterward we dried ourselves and dressed and sat down near the water's edge, feeling clean and tingling soft. Behind our backs the forest was full with growth and life and felt as if it might reach out and pull us in.

"I wish we could go on a canoe trip with Grandpa Nye," I said.

110

"Oh, Vanessa, he's too old now," she said.

"I know, but two Indians could paddle him when he got tired. He *wants* to go," I said. "It makes him sad that . . ." A terrible uneasiness flooded up in me. I looked at Lisa, her lovely profile, as she sat staring innocently out over the water, and I hated her.

On a cold, gray day in early October when we were going to dinner at Grandpa Nye's for the first time, our school car-pool let me off on the way home at the corner of Victory Parkway and Forest Street, and I walked from there to Grandpa Nye's. I'd have nearly two hours alone with him before Mama and Daddy and Lisa arrived, and he had promised he would read me the old DeGolyer manuscript.

The sky was so solidly gray it blended into the gray wet chill of the air; it was a cold that wrapped round my stomach and brought back the feel of childhood—the bleak feeling of being alone, and cold, and very small, my whole skin yellowed with goose-pimples. But then, as I climbed the hill up Salt Lick Avenue, my blood warmed, and when I saw the lights in Grandpa Nye's library window and smelled the fire, a wild excitement swirled in my brain.

111

Grandpa Nye's face was warm and he smelled of his cigar. He was gentle as if part of him were for me and part were still the warm dream mind of the book he was reading.

When we went into the library and sat down, he said, "Well, Vanessa, what are you going to be after you go to college?"

"A writer," I said. I felt myself blushing.

"I used to write short stories for the old *Penny Post* when I was in college," he said, as if he didn't notice. "I sold them for a dollar apiece. Probably 99¢ more than they were worth."

In *The Nye Family Record* he wrote: "While I was still at Farmer's College I became the correspondent on College Hill for the Cincinnati *Gazette*. Then the *Gazette* invited me to spend the Christmas holidays with them in 1881 and '82. The city editor put me in the charge of a reporter, Frank Tunison, and I trotted around with him on his rounds. This was valuable experience, and when my college course was completed in June, 1882, the *Gazette* offered me a job as a reporter at $15.00 a week. So I was spared the grief of hunting for something to do. I went straight from school to the newspaper and began the work of mak-

112

ing a living. I was made a police reporter, and I suppose there never was a greater greenhorn. My life as a boy had been peculiarly sheltered and to be suddenly projected into the world of policemen and criminals, of which I had no previous knowledge, was a fearful change. I survived it, however, and when on January 1, the *Gazette* was consolidated with the *Commercial*, I became a general reporter. Mr. Murat Halstead, the editor, was exceedingly kind to me. He sent me in the summer of 1883, in the campaign when Foraker ran against Hoadley for the Governorship, to write a letter from each one of the eighty-eight counties in Ohio—a letter a day. That was a most enjoyable experience. It gave me a knowledge of the geography, history, and people of Ohio that otherwise I would have never gained.

"On January 1, 1884, I became City Editor of the *Times Star.*"

"When he was only twenty-two," Daddy told me once

"Which position," Grandpa Nye wrote, "I held until 1890 when I gave it up to devote my time to lecturing. I had a growing family and there was more money in lecturing, but the more successful I became in the lecturing business, the more I was away from home, so in 1894 when Mr. Morgan Burke offered me a position in his firm, I accepted it."

"The Morgan Burke Company bought and sold pig iron, coke, and coal," Daddy explained to me. "They bought in the South, sold in the North, and owned a great foundry down the river as well as mines and little blast furnaces all over the South with names like the Princess, the Bessie, etc.

"Morgan Burke made Papa his partner, and after Morgan Burke was killed in a train accident down near Nashville in 1904, Papa took over the business and ran it single-handed until . . ."

"What?" I asked.

"I don't feel like talking about it right now," Daddy said, turning away.

"The men on the Chautauqua Circuit were a special breed, rather like actors," Uncle Charles told me one time. "Every once in a while one of them came to our house to dinner. They were the only men I ever knew who called Papa 'Natty.'"

Grandpa Nye lectured all over the Midwest and parts of the South, accompanying his lectures with "Magnificent Dissolving Stereopticon Views." He lectured on "Washington, City of Magnificent Distances," on "Lincoln, the Great Emancipator," on "Emerson and Concord," on "Hawthorne, Whittier, and Holmes," on "Irving and the Hudson," on "The Western Writers"—the Cary Sisters, the Piatts, Harriet Beecher Stowe, W. H. Venable, Thomas Buchanan Read, and Madame Trollope. He went to Europe and prepared lectures on "The People of London," on "Edinburgh and Bits of Scotland," on "Views Afoot in Ireland," as well as "A Bird's-Eye View of France."

His lectures were immensely successful. Of his lecture on "The American Gibraltar"—Quebec—the Omaha *Bee* said, "A finer and more stirring lecture could not be delivered in America." The *Enquirer* said, "His account of kissing the Blarney stone brought down the house." When she was very old, my Great-Aunt Sarah, Mama's aunt, told me she remembered very clearly someone running up to her as she stood on the steps of Hughes High School and saying in great excitement, "Mr. *Nye* is giving a lecture tonight."

Now in his library Grandpa Nye got up from his green velvet chair and crossed the room to put another log on the fire. I looked at his shoulders which were bent and strong from years of chopping wood, paddling canoes, lifting logs. "I haven't found it difficult to grow old," he said, straightening up. "It's strange, but I don't have the slightest realization that I will soon be seventy-nine. I think I felt older at twenty-one than I do now.

"In life there are disappointments and sorrows," he said when he sat down again. "No one escapes them. But one can never be lonely when he has the fields and the forest, the rivers and lakes for his companions. They never seemed to me to be inanimate things; rather they are living things. So the Indians thought, as well. And one can never be lonely or lack employment when he has a good book. Next to the love I bear nature is my love for books. I am no bookworm. No dry and dusty student. But all my life I have read, and books are still as much a delight to me as when I discovered my first book—*The Arabian Nights*. So fascinating was that book that I could not lay it aside. I remember I devoured it by the light of a kerosene lamp when I went to bed and was supposed to be sleeping. Perhaps it was then I acquired the bad habit I have of reading in bed. . . ."

"Oh, I used to read like that," I said. "Mama would call upstairs and ask if my light was out, and I didn't want to lie so I'd call back, 'What?' while I turned off the light. The she'd ask a second time, and I'd say 'Yes,' and try to sound very sleepy, but afterwards sometimes I'd start reading again with my flashlight."

In my brain for an instant there was a quiver from the memory of being in a dark, profound, passionate state reading *Little Jeannie of France* when I was seven. I was sitting in the living room on a straight chair, reading, and they came and told me supper was ready. Then they came and stood over me saying they knew I could hear them saying, "Vanessa, supper is ready." They went away. I was near the end and my heart was breaking. When I finished, I threw my book down on the floor and I threw myself down on top of it, sobbing violently.

Grandpa Nye said, "When I was sixteen my father introduced me to Macaulay's essays, and to the *Lays of Ancient Rome*. These were a pleasure beyond words. He loved Southey's ballads, many of which he knew by heart. He also had me read Milton and Shakespeare. So it was early in life that I began to read books of merit. And yet I love all books. Sometimes I think I am entirely lacking in taste. I read everything. In reading all is grist that comes to my mill.

117

"In one area only have I concentrated. I don't know how many years ago I became interested in local history. Probably I was always interested in it, and this interest gradually increased until I made it a definite object of study. As a result I accumulated my great collection of Harrisoniana. The collection is notable for its extent and completeness. There are 1,600 titles in my catalogue of it, and it is of the more moment because practically all the books are annotated; that is, I have written about them, and what I wrote is inserted in each book.

"In reality this collection is the history of the Ohio Valley between the years 1791 and 1841; for in November, 1791, William Henry Harrison, then a young ensign in the army, arrived at Cincinnati as the remnants of St. Clair's slaughtered army were making their way through the forest to seek shelter behind the walls of Fort Washington. Only the Indian love of loot saved their lives.

> "But by the yellow Tiber
> Was tumult and affright!"

Grandpa Nye shouted the lines and then said quietly, "Never did Lars Porsena so terrify Rome as the

118

people of Cincinnati were terrified in that dread November of 1791.

"And in January, 1841, William Henry Harrison, who had been elected ninth President of the United States and was then a man of seventy years, stood on the deck of the steamer *Ben Franklin* and bade farewell to the joyous crowd gathered on the public landing, in the windows of houses beyond, and on the rooftops. He spoke of the contrast between the happy prospect before him and the dense and dark forest which had clothed the shores of the Ohio when he arrived on that very spot fifty years before; he spoke of how in 1791 when he first arrived at Cincinnati, he with his small command took shelter in the desolate cabin of a pioneer named Cox, who had cleared his fields, planted his corn, but ere it was harvested, had his life and hopes together ended by the unerring rifle of his ambushed foe.

"There is no complete record of the speech General Harrison gave that morning, but we know that in conclusion he said, 'Gentlemen and Fellow Citizens, perhaps this may be the last time I may have the pleasure of speaking to you on earth or seeing you. I will bid you farewell; if forever, fare thee well.' The steamboat pulled out. The crowd shouted with joy, and General Harrison from the deck waved his tall beaver hat in farewell.

"As the *Ben Franklin* steamed slowly up the Ohio, farmers came down to the riverbank where fifty years before Indians had lurked, ready to shoot if an ark drew close; the farmers fired their guns in the air, threw up their hats and shouted, 'Huzza for old Tip, the People's President of the West!' Crowds waved flags, and at every important place there was a reception. One young man, John Findlay Torrence, wrote that General Harrison's arm was almost shook off by the time he reached Wheeling, but the people must be pleased, therefore he gave them the left, then the right.

"Six months later the same people, now sad and silent, gathered to pay their last homage as the steamer *Raritan* bore the President in his casket down the noble river to his final resting place. Everywhere were the now gray-bearded pioneers. At Cincinnati old weather-beaten soldiers marched around the hearse. In severe suffering these soldiers as young men had followed the General in his brilliant campaigns of 1812 and 1813 to his country's battles and to victory. At North Bend the country people for miles around came to pay their last tribute of respect. They formed a great procession, and bore the casket to a vault of native stone on top of a knoll overlooking the Ohio near the General's residence. When at last the door of the tomb was closed, and the long summer day —July 7, 1841—had come to an end, darkness fell and the multitude dispersed leaving the dead to sleep on the shores of the Ohio which fifty years before had carried him to the frontier, river which had carried him on his last earthly journey, river of eternal mystery."

Upstairs in the room where Grandpa Nye had spent so many years working on *Old Tippecanoe: The Life and Times of William Henry Harrison*, there were here and there among the books that lined the walls, old engravings of scenes from Harrison's life and mementos of that wild campaign of 1840, including, for instance, the cover of the sheet music for the "Log Cabin or Tippecanoe Quick Step"; but it was not Harrison's presence I felt in the room, rather it was the dark Tecumseh's. Sometimes he almost seemed to be there in a corner of the room, breathing. And when I walked around the room, looking into the heavy gray atmosphere of the old engravings, it was to Tecumseh that I was drawn; and more than to any picture to the photograph of the rock with the inscription which said:

Here
October 5, 1813
was fought
The Battle of the Thames
and here
Tecumseh fell.

"Tecumseh went into battle that day at the Thames knowing that he would not survive it; yet he was determined to fight or die in the effort," Grandpa Nye told me one time. "The British were placed in a grove of trees on a hill above the north bank of the Thames, the Indians in a swamp beyond the hill. When Harrison's cavalry attacked, the British, after just a few minutes, laid down their arms and surrendered. General Proctor, at the rear, fled, and was later court-martialed for this disgrace. In the swamp the Indians, led by Tecumseh, raised the battle cry. They held their line and fought on. All day above the din of arms Tecumseh's voice could be heard animating them to deeds worthy of their race, and when his voice was no longer heard, the Indians, too, fled.

"Four men claimed the honor of having shot him. It was said the Kentuckians scalped him. The Indians in Moravian Town hinted darkly that he was buried under water.

"Yet it was also reported that even in death Tecumseh's countenance betrayed his lofty spirit.

"He was a brave and humane man, a man of genius with a strong and noble character. He was a Shawnee—the first of the great Ohio men in history; and he was filled with the dream that the Indians could be saved if he could form a firm federation of all the Indian tribes, if the Indians would also give up alcohol and white man's dress, stop trading with white men, and stop marrying the white renegades who brought disease and corrupted the morals of the tribes. It had been the dream of Pontiac as well, and to this end Tecumseh devoted his energy and his great organizing abilities. For a period of more than fifteen years after he was made chief in 1795, Tecumseh was ever on the move extending his influence—now on the Wabash, now on the Mississippi, now on the Plains beyond, now at Vincennes confronting Governor William Henry Harrison. He had great intellectual power and a gift for oratory which was both persuasive and sublime and enabled him as he governed in the field so to prescribe in the council. In his plan for a vast continental confederacy he had accomplished far more than Pontiac had even dreamed when his—Tecumseh's—brother, the Prophet, against Tecumseh's express command to avoid a battle at any cost, attacked Harrison's forces before dawn on November 7, 1811, near the place where the Prophet had established his town for young warriors at the juncture of the Tippecanoe and the Wabash.

"There is no doubt that Tecumseh meant to fight it out. But he was not ready. He was in the South with the Creek and Cherokee Nations at the time of the Battle of Tippecanoe. And when he came home, his hopes ruined forever, he was seized with a sudden anger. He grabbed his brother and shook him as a terrier shakes a rat. There was nothing left for Tecumseh to do but go over to the British. They made him a brigadier general, and then they, too, by their cowardice betrayed him.

"No tall shaft rises by the Thames to tell the story of the battle as at the Tippecanoe, but the traditions of the place are all Tecumseh's, and by the side of the road which is now the main road between Detroit and Toronto, there is a block of chipped granite with this inscription:

Here
October 5, 1813
was fought
The Battle of the Thames
and here
Tecumseh fell."

Grandpa Nye and I sat a few moments in silence, and then he offered me a cigar, and took one himself. I bit off the end of mine, accepted his light, and puffed a terrible cloud of smoke.

He said, "My Grandfather Nye at Sherbrooke in the Province of Quebec preached a sermon at the time of Harrison's death, using as his text a portion of the thirty-eighth verse of the third chapter of II Samuel—'There is a prince and a great man has fallen in Israel.' My grandfather was a man of broad views, of a kindly disposition, and his sermon does him credit."

Then Grandpa Nye looked directly at me and said,

125

"The blood of your forebears which runs in your veins is good blood. Excepting, of course, that of your pirate ancestor on your Grandmother Nye's side of the family.

"That reminds me, Vanessa. I was going to read you the old DeGolyer manuscript today."

"Yes," I said. "You promised."

He smiled and leaned forward and from the pile of books on his desk, he pulled a slim volume bound in dark blue leather.

"I knew nothing at all about the existence of this manuscript," he said, "until about the year 1900 when your Uncle Ben called on Mother's cousin, Laura DeGolyer, the daughter of David Lee, in Evanston, and she produced this manuscript for him to read. It tells the story of the life of the first DeGolyer, James, as it was related by his son, Joseph, when he was an old man, to his son, David Lee DeGolyer, who committed it to writing in the old farmhouse at Broadalbin on January 17, 1839. David Lee was an older brother of my grandfather, Hezekiah Gordon DeGolyer, who met his death while sailing through the Straits of Mackinac in the summer of 1862—the summer before I was born, you know. Your Uncle Ben made a copy of the old manuscript which he sent to me, and I have, since, added in certain information—matters of record—as well as a few touches from the story that came down to us by word of mouth through the generations."

Then without further ado Grandpa Nye said in stentorian tones, "Hear then the story of the life of the grandfather of my Grandfather DeGolyer." And he read:

"Broadalbin, January 17, 1839
Mr. Joseph DeGolyer, Esquire
Related the following with regard to his father:

"First, he says that his father, James DeGolyer, was born in France and while still quite young he left his father's house unknown to his father and enlisted in the French Army. The army in which he enlisted was sent to the Province of Lower Canada; he being sent with said army, remained a short time with the army in Canada, and then left that army without leave and came to the United Colonies of Great Brit ain, since called the United States of America, and settled in the state of Massachusetts, where he lived a short time and learned to speak the English language. He married a wife in said state by the name of

Jane Hatch by whom he had five sons and two daughters. The names of the sons were as follows, beginning at the oldest: John, James, Joseph, Anthony, and Abel DeGolyer, who are all dead with the exception of the narrator. The names of the daughters were Mary and Lydia DeGolyer, the latter only living, leaving only a son and a daughter living (in 1839). Joseph DeGolyer now being 76 years old in December 23, and Lydia DeGolyer now being 69 years old; said Joseph being a farmer and living in the county of Montgomery, State of New York, in which place he has lived about fifty years; and Lydia, his sister, living in the county and state aforesaid. John DeGolyer died about twenty years since. James DeGolyer, Jr., died in March, 1838. Anthony DeGolyer died about three years since in the State of Ohio, and Abel about five years since. The daughter Mary, have not heard what time she died, but she died somewhere in the State of Ohio.

"Further, Joseph DeGolyer says that Jane DeGolyer, his mother, died 55 years since, in the year, 1784, and is buried by the Mohawk River. His father, James DeGolyer, he does not know as certain where he died or what time, but presumes that he is dead beyond a doubt.

"Second: Joseph DeGolyer states that he last saw his father about 54 years since, and that he was then about 55 years old which would bring him to be born about the year 1730 in the city of Paris, the son of Anthony DeGolyer. In France the name was spelled 'de Gaullier,' and he was of a noble family. Joseph DeGolyer says that his father was an excellent Latin scholar and of extraordinary intelligence, and that he was being educated for the priesthood very much against his will. It was therefore that while still quite young he left his father's house unknown to his father and enlisted in the army. He was immediately ordered to Flanders under the command of General Lowendahl and there in the battle at the city of Bergen op Zoom he received a severe wound that nearly cost him his life.

"Joseph DeGolyer says that he often heard his father speak of this battle, that it was a severe conflict in the city of Bergen op Zoom in the country then called Flanders, since called Holland, that one after another eight platoons were sent to scale a certain wall, and each was cut down like so much grass. At length a ninth platoon was sent out and this one succeeded in gaining a footing on the wall, but his father, James DeGolyer, being in this ninth platoon, was struck a severe blow with a broad sword. The sword struck his head and, as it turned out, opened his skull and exposed his brains to view. After the battle he was about to be placed with hundreds of other unfortunate ones in the open trenches for burial, but a spark of life was observed, and he was carried instead to the hospital.

"There when he recovered consciousness, the surgeon handed him a mirror and said, 'Young man, if you live, you can say you have seen your own brains.' Joseph DeGolyer says his father often told this story.

"Also Joseph DeGolyer says that he has seen this wound frequently, for it never healed properly and it bothered his father ever after, especially in stormy weather, though he never knew his father to be complaining of sickness. He says that his father was, on the contrary, of a healthy countenance; he was brave, restless, intelligent, strong, and strong-willed. He was about five foot eight in height, and of a rather dark complexion.

"Further, Joseph DeGolyer says that when the army in which his father enlisted was sent to Canada, he went with it, for he dared not return home for fear of his father, that he would put him in a monastery or some other place of confinement.

"He says it was shortly after the peace of Aix-la-Chapelle that his father was sent to Canada and that there he remained a short time, probably two years or three. He was there long enough to gain some knowledge of the Indian languages and of the wilderness as will be seen in the story that follows.

"He was a good skater and was frequently sent to carry messages over the ice in winter time from one point to another; and in the spring and summer he served as a scout. He was on a scouting expedition with two Indians when he proposed to hire them as guides to conduct him across the wilderness to the English Colonies. They were but a few days gone south into the forest when he overheard the foxy Indians plotting to secure a reward by leading him back to the French. That night he lay awake watching for his opportunity, and when the Indians were fast asleep he tomahawked them both.

"Alone and unguided he continued his journey. After three weeks wandering in the wilderness he came upon a pioneer clearing where he found a man working in a field. He explained to him, as best he could by signs and in broken English, his situation. He was weak from starvation, and the pioneer took him in and fed him broth until he became strong enough to take other food, and finally to continue on his journey.

"He made his way south following the valley of the Connecticut River and then east by the Bay Path as far as the town of Woodstock in the State of Massachusetts, now in Connecticut, and there he found some French families, the remnants of a French Huguenot colony which had been massacred in the nearby town of Oxford in the Indian War of the previous century. There he stopped. He learned the English language, and there in the neighboring town of Sturbridge he met Jane, the daughter of Joseph Hatch and Lydia Cottle Hatch, farmers, and they were married in February, 1753.

"They lived on a farm next to her father's farm on the Old Indian Path from 1753 to 1756 when, after the outbreak of war between the French and English, they removed west to Stockbridge and lived there among the friendly Housatonic Indians, later called Stockbridge Indians. He says that his father hunted with these Indians and learned their language and in that war now called the Old French War or the French and Indian War, he served as a scout.

"Mary the first daughter was born at Sturbridge in 1753, and John, the first son, was also born at Sturbridge; and after that while they lived at Stockbridge James DeGolyer, Jr., was born.

"There was a circumstance which took place during that war in 1757 or about that time, which is worthy of being recorded. James DeGolyer was stationed at what was then called Fort George at the southeast end of Lake George. On a certain day 25 men were sent out on what was called a scouting party. The first day after leaving the fort, the company encamped on the bank of Lake George. Very early the next morning the Indians and French from Canada, in large numbers, fell upon them and killed 20 of them on the ground. James DeGolyer, being an early riser, had gone previous to the attack down to the lake to wash himself. When he found how it was going with those in the camp, he waded out into the water, but being discovered, he was ordered to come out. He and four more were taken for prisoners and they started for Canada. That night after they were encamped, the five prisoners were bound with moosewood bark, their backs to the trees, their hands tied behind them, as was customary in such cases. Pine splinters and other fuel were piled about their feet, and around their legs. Then the Indians had a great dance over their victory. After their dance, as usual, they fell asleep. All were asleep except the prisoners. At this critical time, James DeGolyer began working his arms in such manner as to peel the skin from his wrists, which caused the blood to run freely, which caused the moosewood bark to stretch, by which means he got his hands loose. He then got his knife, which the Indians had overlooked, and cut his feet loose. He then very carefully drew from the sleeping sentry his gun. Just then another prisoner exclaimed loudly in great terror, 'James, turn me loose,' and thus awakened the Indians. James De-Golyer made the best of his way back to the fort. He was the only one of the 25 who returned to Fort George to tell the sad fate of his comrades—20 of them massacred on the ground as they slept, and four burned alive by the Indians at sunrise the following day. He was nine seasons in the French War.

"The family remained until after the struggle over the possession of Canada at Stockbridge from whence they removed to Kinderhook in Columbia County, New York, and later to a place on the Mohawk River in the Woestina, meaning wilderness in Dutch. In Kinderhook the four youngest children were born—Joseph (the narrator) on December 23,

1762, and Anthony, Lydia, and Abel, in that order all between the years 1762 and 1772.

"Joseph DeGolyer says that his father was a man of mysterious mien, different in appearance from the English and Dutch settlers. He has often heard that his father was a French nobleman. He did not become a farmer, but he made the living for the family by the sale of furs and by trading with the Indians. He liked to go off into the forest, hunting, for days at a time; he lodged overnight with the Indians in their villages; he learned several Indian languages and studied their lore. He was drawn to the Indians, and to the wilderness, and to the life on the border between the white man and the Indians. When the family moved to the place on the Mohawk River in the Schenectady patent, they were close to Mohawk Indian settlements.

"Joseph DeGolyer further states that during the time they lived at Kinderhook and later when they lived on the Mohawk River, before the War of the Revolution broke out, his father went on several expeditions to the west to trade with the Indians at Michilimackinac. He was gone then for many months, going once, as he recalls, with a young man of Dutch descent and his Negro slave. These expeditions were made by bark canoe up the Mohawk to Oneida Lake, then following its outlet to Oswego, and from there along the shores of Lake Ontario to Lake Erie. James DeGolyer beheld the falls at Niagara, and spoke of their wild grandeur on his return. He followed the shore of Lake Erie to Detroit, then proceeded up that river, and along the shores of Lake Huron to Michilimackinac, where he traded with the Indian for his furs. He recalls his father speaking of the beauty of those far lakes, of their vastness, and the wilderness there, the Indians, the forests of pine, of birch, the luminous forests of beech, and his mother saying sadly she had come so far into the wilderness already. She never complained, nor of sickness, but as the years went on she slowly tired."

Grandpa Nye looked up and said, "The first years they lived by the Mohawk River, Sir William Johnson, who was for many years the Superintendent of Indian Affairs, kept the peace with the Six Nations, as he had for years. He was beloved of the Indians. He had learned the Mohawk language and they adopted him. They called him "Waraghiyaghey.' He died in 1774, and his son, Sir John Johnson, lured the Indians to the British side by misrepresenting the American cause to them. He encouraged the Indians in their frightful massacres at Cherry Valley, at Wyoming, Harpersfield, German Flats; and he tried to lure the settlers in the Mohawk Valley to the British side by threats of massacres, by promises of safety, and other rewards. Many settlers did in fear join the Tories. Others fled the region to safety. From Lake Champlain south nearly every settlement was desolated. Nearly every family lost some of its members."

Grandpa Nye looked off into space for a moment and then resumed his reading.

"Joseph DeGolyer states that his father, James DeGolyer, was the first in the family to enlist in the militia; and did so in March 1776. He enlisted in the regiment of Colonel Marinus Willet. Shortly after his father enlisted, James DeGolyer, Jr., enlisted, then John, then himself, Joseph, he being then 16 years old, Anthony and Abel being then too young, remained home with their mother and their sisters. All fought in the region of the Mohawk Valley save for James DeGolyer, Jr. And he achieved a certain fame for he was stationed at West Point, and he guarded the spy Major André and loaned him his Bible on the eve of his execution.

"Joseph DeGolyer says he was in the same company with his father, and he often went with him on scouting parties in an effort to prevent the country from surprise attack. He recalls two battles in particular: in one they marched with Colonel Willet from Fort Schuyler and took part in the frightful conflict at Oriskany; and the second, a battle at Klock's Flats, where again they were victorious in the struggle against the forces of Sir John Johnson and Joseph Brant. In regard to these battles he remembers the saying that the only sadder thing than defeat is victory, for the victors must bury the dead.

"He says further that after his father's term of enlistment expired, he enlisted again in Colonel Willet's company, and that in return for this second term of enlistment his father was to receive, instead of pay, 200 acres of bounty land, and that this land was indeed granted to him. This land was at a place called White Creek on the western shore of Lake Champlain.

"But not long after his father returned home at the end of the war, his mother, Jane DeGolyer, died. She was buried by the Mohawk River in the year 1784. His father removed to the land on the shore of Lake Champlain, taking with him only Abel, all the other children being then grown or married. After some years Abel returned to live with him (Joseph) and help him with clearing the land on his farm. From that time on his father lived isolated from his children. Nothing definite is known about him since the year 1790 except that he did not remain at Lake Champlain. Joseph has heard that his father married again but that this second wife did die shortly after their marriage, and his father sold his land soon thereafter and went to the West to live among the Indians in the country beyond Michilimackinac. He has also heard that his father lived to the age of 97 years at the time of his death. This is only a report, but he is inclined to believe in its truth. It was about a dozen years since he received this report of the death of his father whom he had presumed dead many years previous.

"Joseph DeGolyer wishes to state that thus his father fought in three wars over a span of more than 35 years. The War of the Austrian Succession, in which he fought for France; the French and Indian War, in which he fought for American and British interests; and the War of the American Revolution, in which he fought for American Independence. One could rightly say he was a warrior, and, too, that James DeGolyer, emigrant, was a true American patriot and defender of the Declaration of Indepen-

139

dence, for when the war broke out in the Mohawk Valley, he was one of the first to join the militia, and he persuaded his three eldest sons to join as well, and this at a time when they were surrounded without by savages bent on their destruction and within by Tories who tried every means to lure them to the British side.

"Joseph DeGolyer believes it was this fearful time did shorten his mother's life and leave his brave father at the war's end bereft. He thinks that had she not died his father would have kept the land granted him at White Creek, but he thinks it was his father's nature that he would leave it after a few years, selling it for whatever he could get, to go west through the forest and across the lakes he so loved, to end his days among the Indians in the wilderness.

"As for himself, Joseph, he says that about five years after the close of the War of the Revolution, he purchased the land for his farm at Broadalbin, then called Fonda's Bush, on the site of the former Indian village of Caughnawaga. He married and began the work of clearing the land and building his house. His younger brother Anthony remained with him, living in his house a number of years and helping him with the work of clearing the land, as did Abel also later for a time. Anthony married Patty Willis and they had a son, James DeGolyer, and after her death he married Hannah Willis, and in the year 1806 they removed to the State of Ohio, and there he cleared the land for his farm and built his house, and he died there and is buried as he, Joseph, has been informed, on a hill overlooking the Miami river. He, Joseph DeGolyer, married Cornelia Bone in the year 1789. Their first born son James DeGolyer died in 1792 when he was but three years old. Their daughters were Catherine and Jane. Cornelia Bone died in January 1796 and is buried with her people. In the year 1797 he, Joseph DeGolyer, married Hannah Lee by whom he had 13 children in this order: John, Ann, James, Eunice, William, Elizabeth, Joseph, David Lee, Hannah, Hezekiah Gordon, Calvin, Harriet, and Fannie. Of these all are living (in 1839) save his daughter Ann who lived with him on the farm and died unmarried in the year 1834, and is buried on the farm, as he, Joseph, will be, and his wife, Hannah, and those of his children who so desire, on this land he cleared and cultivated and lived on for 50 years, and more."

Grandpa Nye put the bound manuscript down on his desk. His weathered old Indian face looked sad.

141

He swallowed. "The blood of your forebears which runs in your veins is good blood," he said.

He was quiet a minute and then he said, "The life of the pioneer was one of hard work, hard, back-breaking, never-ending work, and that life fell to the children of the first James DeGolyer—to Joseph, to Anthony, to their sister Mary, who died somewhere in the State of Ohio. Joseph DeGolyer rose to be a man of substance and standing in the community, but the hardship of his life is in the language of this narrative. The pioneer had to have character; he had to keep going; he had to endure poverty, and he could not weaken. Joseph felt a certain awe of his father who remained mysterious, exotic—a warrior, a hunter, a man intoxicated by the forest which stretched unbroken a thousand miles from a few hundred miles inland as far as the prairie. I imagine that the American forest, its very vastness, its grandeur caused in James DeGolyer a certain rapture such as that felt by Chateaubriand or, later, by Francis Parkman who envisioned it as it had been: 'The forest full of game; the ducks, the geese, and partridges; the prodigious flocks of wild pigeons that darkened the air; the bears; the beavers; and above all the Indians, their canoes, dress, ball play, and dances.' And so this

James went to end his days far from his children in that country beyond Michilimackinac, and in the twilight of his life, sat listening, as I imagine, through the long winter evenings to Chippewa legends such as those set down by Henry Rowe Schoolcraft—wonderful, human magic tales replete with wild forest notions of spiritual agencies, necromancy, and demonology."

Later, after Mama and Daddy and Lisa arrived, Grandpa Nye said, "You know, Vanessa, don't you, that it was from the Ojibway legends as Schoolcraft set them down that Longfellow took his Hiawatha—not realizing, apparently, when he chose the Iroquois Hiawatha rather than the Ojibway Manabozho that the languages and cultures of the Iroquois and the Algonquin Indians were as different from each other as Chinese and English."

Mama's eyes shone blue and she began to recite, joined by all —

> By the shores of Gitche Gumee
> By the shining Big-Sea-Water . . .

At dinner that night while we drank his wine and ate a roast of beef, Grandpa Nye told the story of the

143

time he held the lion in his arms. "Many years ago on the Fourth of July, 1876," he began, "a balloonist made an ascension from the Cincinnati Zoo and took along a baby lion as an added attraction. On that sunny Fourth, Ben and I and our friends were swimming at the Dayton Sandbar on the Kentucky side of the Ohio. We were swimming naked, of course," Grandpa Nye said. "We looked up and saw a huge silver balloon, with ribbons floating around the basket, drifting downward and about to fall in the river. It landed in a foot or two of water at the edge of the bar, and we boys rushed to grab the basket. The aeronaut was half frightened to death and pale as a sheet. The lion jumped out. It was about the size of a large police dog, and as the poor thing started to trot off across the sand, I ran after it and caught it. It was quite tame and seemed to enjoy being held in my arms. And that," concluded Grandpa Nye, "is the only time I ever held a lion in my arms."

But years later in France he did go up in a balloon. He was preparing "A Bird's-Eye View of France" for the series of lectures he gave in 1891 and 1892. When the balloon passed over the chateau of a famous duke, the duke came out on the terrace and called up, "Come down, come down for lunch!" But Grandpa

Nye just doffed his hat and sailed on through the wonderful upper regions of the atmosphere.

After supper Lisa and I went round looking at the old pictures in the upstairs hall, and as we stood in front of a picture of Grandpa Nye and William Howard Taft, I imagined Grandpa Nye up there in the balloon's basket, floating by, looking just as he did in the picture in his high silk hat and his Prince Albert coat, with a smile on his face and a debonair tilt to his head. In the picture, which was taken in 1915, he was handing the trowel to William Howard Taft to lay the cornerstone of the new Hamilton County Courthouse. The old courthouse had been gutted by fire during the Courthouse Riot of 1884, the courthouse rebuilt had proved inadequate, and Grandpa Nye had been appointed head of the commission to build the new courthouse. Taft, who had finished his term as the twenty-seventh President and hadn't yet been appointed to his seat as Chief Justice, wore a bowler and had a genial expression, with his white walrus mustache and a rose in his buttonhole. He was very wide; he took up two thirds of the picture and Grandpa Nye stood sidewise.

In the picture Grandpa Nye looked so much like Daddy I would have thought it was Daddy except he wasn't wearing Daddy's silver-rimmed glasses. Once later when I remarked the uncanny resemblance, Mama said, "It's the charm. The Nyes—they all have it."

Mama touched Daddy's back, and he, pleased, recalled the time when he was little and Taft was President and the President came to dinner. "Papa said to me, 'Morgan, will you speak to the President?' I spoke to the President," Daddy said. "He ate voluminously, but very neatly."

Lisa and I moved on to look at the picture next to Grandpa Nye and William Howard Taft. Five women and one man and a boy were all on camelback in the desert. Behind them loomed a sphinx and a pyramid. The women were sitting sidesaddle in their long skirts and their huge puffed sleeves; their shoes were just peeking out from under their skirts. The boy was twelve or thirteen and he had large eyes. The man wore a big, dark, old-fashioned mustache and a very big white desert hat.

Daddy came upstairs and stopped beside us. He said it was taken on the famous trip when Uncle George, his great-uncle George DeGolyer, went around the world with the five DeGolyer sisters— Daddy's grandmother and his great-aunts Eda, Belle,

146

Kate, and Jenny—and Uncle Andrew. "That was in 1892 and '93, the year after your Great-Grandfather Joab Nye's death," Daddy said. "Your great-grandmother, Vanessa DeGolyer Nye, had been left a widow, and then that same summer their house on College Hill was struck by lightning and burned to the ground."

In *The Nye Family Record* Grandpa Nye wrote: "Though my father became a successful man of business, he retained his scholarly quiet ways. He read Latin and Greek at sight and he spoke French fluently. He graduated from McGill in the year 1861, the valedictorian of his class, and after he and Mother were married he taught Latin. He was a fine teacher. In May of 1872 we removed to Cincinnati, and Father joined the firm of Queen City Carriages, of which he was treasurer at the time of his death. We lived in College Hill and Father rode to and from the city on the old narrow-gauge railway. He always carried a book, for he was an omnivorous reader. On the second of July, 1892, he had with him Hardy's *Tess of the D'Urbervilles*. He was down at the Gest Street Station of the old C.H.&D., waiting for the train on which he was accustomed to ride home in the evening, and, absorbed in reading *Tess*, he started across the tracks,

147

as was his wont. He did not hear the switch engine that bore down on him, though they said they rang the bell. He died without regaining consciousness two hours later at the Cincinnati Hospital, where the ambulance had taken him.

"His death came to us not only as a shock but as a profound sorrow. He was a lovable man, devoted to my mother and to his children, and we all grieved for him. To this day, I mourn him and feel that his death, in his fifty-fifth year, was a calamity. Life for him was so full and he enjoyed it so much that I could never dismiss the feeling that in some way he had missed the years that would have been the sweetest to him. As I write this, I am many years older than he was when he died, yet I always think of him as much older than I am or older than I could be; that is, years have not changed the relation of parent and child."

"He was a most affectionate man," Uncle Charles told me. "He was very kind with children. He was beloved throughout the city. Years after his death when people heard my name, they spoke to me of my grandfather. I remember Papa coming in to wake us in the morning, and he was weeping. I never knew before that grown men wept. Then he told us our Grandfather Nye had died in the night."

In *The Nye Family Record* Grandpa Nye wrote, "After my father's death, the commodious new residence he had built was struck by lightning, which set fire to the roof, and the whole house was destroyed. All the furniture, the books, and the bric-a-brac were consumed. These were the accumulations of many years, and the clothing, too, was destroyed, so my mother was left with only the clothes on her back. After Father's death, Uncle George and Aunt Jenny had taken over the house, and Mother lived with them. The destruction of the house made them all so unhappy that they determined not to attempt to rebuild or to keep house again. They took a trip around the world, and were gone for more than a year."

"Yes," Daddy said, coming closer to scrutinize the picture, "this was probably taken early in the year 1893 on that famous trip." Then he tried to figure out for us which of his great aunts was which. He mumbled. "No, no, this one must be Eda," he said, pointing. "She was the one who always smelled of perfumes and powders. She was John Randall's grandmother." He mumbled again. "No, *this* is Belle," he said. "She was the one with the thick ankles." (I couldn't see her ankles in the picture.) "This one is Kate. I despised her. De*spised* her. She was an

149

artist, you know. She had a studio in the old Chelsea building in New York. She didn't like people. She had a harsh female voice. And she married *no one*. I refused to go to her funeral."

He paused, and then he said, smiling, "Now, this is Aunt Jenny. She and Uncle George were husband and wife, and they were also first cousins, you know. When they were children, they always said they were going to get married. I suppose everyone just thought it was charming. Certainly no one took it seriously. Then one day when they were sixteen they went off together down the road until they came to a justice of the peace. It was much easier to get married in those days. They came back home for supper and announced that they were married, and that was that.

"Now, this is my grandmother, Vanessa. She was a wonderful woman, wonderful. She loved people. She fought for women's rights in the days when women didn't do such things. She corresponded with Lucy Stone. She was responsible, you know, for having the NO SPITTING signs installed in the streetcars of Cincinnati. Once she was ridiculed in the papers for appearing before the City Council to demand playgrounds for the city's children. The headlines said she said, SANDPILES CURE BOWLEGS. And this," Daddy said gently, pointing to the boy, "is Uncle Andrew. Do you remember him?"

"Oh, Daddy, of course. I loved him so much," I said.

Uncle Andrew was nearly twenty years younger than his oldest brother, Grandpa Nye, and he always seemed to be one of the children with us. One time, I sat next to him at dinner at Grandpa Nye's and I told him something disgusting to try to make him unable to eat. And he told me back something five times as disgusting, about a cow he ate in Arizona, that I've never been able to forget.

Uncle Andrew had a big square face and was pale, and he had very big, very pale, blue eyes that looked innocent and startled, and a high wide bumpy forehead, and very curly brown hair cut short and brushed back. His voice was hoarse and it had sadness in it, because, I thought, his wife he loved so much had died. She was a Florodora girl when he met her in New York. He was studying mining engineering at Columbia. He was on the football team in 1902. After they were married he brought her home to Grandpa Nye's. The family disapproved because she was a dancing girl. Daddy said all the family gathered in the library to meet her, and once he looked over and saw her standing alone near a window. As he watched, a tear rolled down her cheek. Daddy hated the family for making Aunt Francie feel that way. She was the most delicate, the most beautiful creature in all the world—so frail and so lovely —and she went with Uncle Andrew in a dugout through the jungles of Guatemala, when he was working for the U.S. Coast and Geodetic Survey, looking for gold. And later she went with him to India. His job was to set up a great pig-iron blast furnace whose dismantling he had overseen in Batelle, Alabama, where it had been built but never used. Uncle Andrew marked and plotted the bricks and the steel, blueprinted the furnace piece by piece, and shipped it on a huge freighter to the Tata Iron Works, near Calcutta, and there he rebuilt it.

But in India Aunt Francie died. Uncle Andrew wandered grieving through Tibet and China, and when, after many years, he came home, he put his hand in his pocket and pulled out a small object, which he held in his palm. "Morgan," he said to Daddy, "look at this!" It was a soybean.

"That would have been about 1924," Daddy said, "and the soybean was relatively unknown here, though it had been grown in China since before written history."

Uncle Andrew married again, but he never stopped grieving for his beautiful Francie who died when she was still so young. He practiced yoga in his back yard in College Hill. And then one morning in 1935 he woke up and put his feet out of bed and died. "Like that!" Daddy said, snapping his finger and thumb.

"He was the replica of his father," Daddy said. "Your great-grandfather, Joab Nye, who was killed, you know, while he was reading *Tess of the D'Urbervilles*." Suddenly Daddy was trembling with anger. "Don't let anyone ever tell you it was not . . ."

"Not what?" I said.

"Not an accident," he said. His lips were twitching with fury.

Later, often in my mind I saw him, my great-grandfather, Joab Nye, tall and gentle and lovable, reading, his blue eyes far off and deep in *Tess of the D'Urbervilles*, walking the hills of England he'd left when he was three, as he crossed the tracks amid the heat and city sounds of a July evening in the Queen City of the West and looked up (his blue eyes Uncle Andrew's eyes), startled, in the moment he was taken from his book and killed.

On Sunday afternoon, December 7, 1941, I was in Janey's car going to our A.T.C. sorority meeting in town when the news—War—came over the radio. We were by the Country Club golf course. We stopped for a moment. The green hood of Janey's Buick was shining in the sun. We drove on to the meeting, not knowing what else to do.

I see myself still that day in the mirror over the buffet, talking to the other girls around the tea table. I was wearing my yellow sweater with a white round-collared blouse; my face was rosy from sunlamp burn. My voice was forced full of enthusiasm. Inside me I harbored a queer sense of emptiness, futility, and embarrassment.

Our lives didn't change until during the heat of May and June we went to the Red Cross after school to fold bandages. We sat at a long polished table in a cool high-ceilinged room, our hair like the hair of the older women, tied back with white cloth, and carefully we folded gauze into squares. The soft gauze at my fingertips made me think of the soldiers—boys just a little older than we, marching to where they would be shot. I wanted to be a nurse and go among them. I would cool their brows with my hands and comfort them. I thought of Wilfred Owen, the *Anthem for Doomed Youth*—

What passing-bells for these who die as cattle?
Only the monstrous anger of the guns.
Only the stuttering rifles' rapid rattle. . . .

In the evening in the front yard, walking barefoot in the grass, I still was saying the *Anthem for Doomed Youth*

Not in the hands of boys, but in their eyes
Shall shine the holy glimmers of good-byes.
The pallor of girls' brows shall be their pall;
Their flowers the tenderness of silent minds,
And each slow dusk a drawing-down of blinds.

I looked up at the face of our house and imagined the blinds drawn down where inside Daddy paced, saying bitterly, "Nor heed the rumble of the distant drum," and Lisa played "Finlandia," which Daddy loved, and Mama's face glowed; her eyes brimmed up with sentiment. The sun was butter in the maple leaves across the drive and in the ivy leaves over the piano.

At Neah that summer Dirk and I sailed the *Annabel Lee* through golden afternoons far out into West Bay, tacking north and west across the bay to reach the bell buoy off Lee's Point, while far off beyond the horizons at the edges of our minds bombs shrieked down from the sky, England burned. Here the sun was liquid light in the moving bay, the wooded shore of Neahatwantah grew smaller, darker, and the chill wind whipped against the sails and through the rigging and blew the spray back on our faces.

Dirk held the tiller. He watched our course, his blue eyes sad and vacant in his long face. His mouth hung a little open.

"Ready about!" he shouted. I crouched down and let out the starboard stay, pulled back the port stay. "Hard-alee!" he called and around we came with a flapping of sails and cold shadow as I let out the port jib sheet, pulled in the starboard jib sheet and held it to fasten as he would direct.

When we reached the bell buoy off Lee's Point and the woods of this far shore were close, we jibed and sailed downwind. We got out the spinnaker and sailed wing and wing on the long, quiet, sun-warm sail to the Island.

I lay out on the poop deck in my bathing suit. Dirk took off his jacket and his sweater. The sun warmed my back and my legs. Bubbles fizzed in the smoothed blue wake. We rolled swiftly forward with the crests of the waves, and the rhythm of the waves and the sun's heat made me languid, soft, and warm.

I looked through my eyelashes at Dirk's wide-shouldered sun-browned back and his soft blond skin, his hairy legs, his hand on the tiller. I felt strange and fiery and jellylike. I moved to sit next to him. I touched his leg by accident. Why wouldn't he put his arm around me? He moved the tiller, guiding us down the wind.

I got the dipper and scooped us drinks of West Bay water and stared into the blue lake, watched the bubbles fizz, and tried to think of something to talk about. When I did, I had to make myself say it: "What courses will you take in college?"

157

He spoke haltingly in his deep, granulated voice. He would take calculus, chemistry, physics, and English and German. He was going to be a chemical engineer. But next summer when he was eighteen he was going to join the Navy and fight for our country. Then after victory he'd return to Yale.

"Oh, Dirk," I said admiringly.

In a while I said, "I had the worst dream one time this winter. You know what I dreamed?"

"What?" he said.

"I dreamed we came back in the summer and West Bay was dried up. There wasn't any water left—just low hills of red-black wrinkled mud. It was cracked and thick and poison. It felt so *horrible*."

"Gee, you know what, I had a dream like that," he said.

"Really?"

"West Bay was dried up when we came back in the summer." He looked at me for an instant. "Isn't that the damnedest thing?" he said.

"Yes," I said. "Yes, it *is*. It *is*."

"Isn't that the damnedest thing," he said again, shaking his head. Pretty soon he started singing in his show-off, off-key way his own version of the "Caisson" song, using the *Annabel Lee*'s number:

"440! Where ere you go, you will always know that the Star Class goes sailing along."

When we reached the red spar off the Island he shouted, "Ready about! Hard-alee!" and around we came. He let me take the tiller and I held our course on the red barn high on a hill on the far side of Bower's Harbor.

At West Bay in the evening when we had our beach party I walked proudly beside Daddy up to the point and back. He was tall in his white summer ducks and his white shirt. He talked, his wrinkly lips moving in their intricate way, and the sunset light darkened his face and his hands. "Churchill drinks the way I do," he told me in a confidential tone. "It enables him to stay on an even keel."

Dirk and I shot watermelon seeds at each other. I pushed his big thick chest. He started to chase me. "Unfairhouse!" I cried, laughing and happy. "Unfair . . . house, Dirk."

Lisa and I raced off, each to climb our pine trees and high up in the tops, smelling the pine smell and listening to the whirr of the wind in the pine needles, we swayed and leaned out, holding on with one hand. "Bahoom!" we called across to each other, "Bahoom!" Dirk and Elihu answered below.

159

"Will you look at the children!" Mama said loudly to Mrs. Monroe down by fire.

Later, side by side in our cots on the sleeping porch, Lisa went to sleep before me, and I lay awake, my feelings wild, and imagined, and listened to the forest blow, and turned miserably, wanting, wanting sleep. But all that summer Dirk didn't kiss me.

One afternoon late in October when we got home from school there was a letter from Dirk in a white envelope with a Yale crest on it. I turned to the second page. He signed it "Love and Kisses." I went into the lavatory by the front door and doubled over. I couldn't breathe. The washstand blazed white in front of my eyes.

I didn't see him until it was summer again. Mama was working at the draft board and no one went to Neah that summer of 1943. I was junior counselor at Camp Claybanks near Glendale, and Dirk came there to see me the night before he went to Chicago to boot camp. It was nearly ten o'clock when he got there, and then we took a walk down the road to the camp entrance. It was a hot moonless night. The dark shapes of the elms loomed against the sky, and the fireflies were like stars in the fragrant fields of hay. He talked haltingly, gently. My hand brushed the

160

hairs on the back of his hand. We walked more slowly. I felt proud of the way my white piqué dress stretched tight across my bosom and because my skin was sunburned and my hair was clean. At the bend in the road we smelled honeysuckle. I stopped. "Oh, smell it, Dirk," I said, sniffing. "Isn't it beautiful?"

He put his arm around my waist. "Gee, Vanessa, you're swell," he said. Then I felt the sweet wet feel of his mouth, the soft quick feel of the life inside him. We put our heads alongside each other, and our arms around each other. I was afraid we might tip over.

When he came in December to spend three days of his furlough with us, he was a sailor in a middy and bell-bottom trousers, and we drank sherry in the kitchen before dinner with Mama and Daddy. We had fun, all together. We sang, "'Bell-bottom trousers and coats of navy blue. He'll climb the rigging like his daddy used to do.'" We did "Who Put the Overalls in Mrs. Murphy's Chowder" the way we used to at Neah, and Dirk and Lisa got red in the face.

Dirk sang lots of new songs in his show-off off-key way; he pumped his arm and beat his foot. His cowlick was sticking up. He sang, "'I'm goin' to buy a paper doll that I can call my own.'" His winter face was pale and pimply; and even while he sang, the sad vacant look was in his eyes. His mouth hung a little open in the silences.

After Mama and Daddy and Lisa went to bed we turned off the lights and sat by the fire in the living room. He sat on the couch and I lay out in his lap in his arms, and his face in the firelight became so handsome, and his mouth became so soft and our mouths were together. We didn't want them apart. There came to his face and his mouth a sharp odor and I breathed it in and my hands felt his back, his neck, his hair, his face, I rubbed my hands on the rough part where he shaved, and I touched his thick, flat chest, and his hands were on my hair, and on my throat, on my clothes for a moment over my breast.

I thought we should move apart. What if Kroupa had to go to the bathroom and Daddy came down to let him out and found us this way? I stood up. "What if Kroupa should have to go out, Dirk?" I said. But I couldn't stand up, there was no blood in my legs, and I had to be back with him, in his arms, kissing him. I looked up at his face bent over me. "Oh, I love you," I said, breathing in the smell of his mouth and his face which was rosy and handsome in the light of the fire.

162

"Look at all of you, Vanessa," he said, "and all I can have is your head."

"Now, Vanessa," Mama said the next day. "Sex is a very beautiful thing."

I looked aside, but I was frozen to the floor in front of her, nearly sick at my stomach with embarrassment.

"But you must be careful, dear," she said. "I wouldn't lie down together because you might get carried away."

Dirk called me up long distance from San Francisco the night before he shipped out.

"I love you, Vanessa," he said.

"I do you too, Dirk," I said very softly. I was afraid Mama would hear and make fun of us.

"After the war," he said, "when I'm twenty-one . . ."

"Ohh . . ." I said. He didn't say anything.

"Good-bye, Dirk," I said.

"Good-bye, Vanessa. You're swell," he said, and hung up, and three weeks later, out in the Pacific where he stood on the deck of his ship, he was hit by a shell. He was buried at sea, May 7, 1944.

163

I shut the door of my room; I drew down the blinds and doubled over.

Mama was home from the draft board. I heard her outdoors in the drive talking to Helen Foster. "And Derek Monroe, his uncle whom he was named for, was killed in France in the *First* World War," Mama said, an awful pleasured wincing in her voice.

And Here
Tecumseh Fell

DECEMBER 22, 1954: Mama and Daddy were standing side by side on the sidewalk waiting for me as I got off the airport limousine. Mama's blue eyes were shining, and her skin was soft and pale with a silvery blush to it, and Daddy, with his long hooked nose and his silver rimmed glasses, looked tall and well-dressed in his gray felt hat, his gray tweed coat, his kid gloves. They seemed so brave and sad going through life side by side like that. I was going to cry, but I held my love in my throat and hugged them lightheartedly.

"How are you, darling?" Mama said.

"I'm fine," I said. I was home after a year from graduate school in California.

"How is Grandpa Nye?" I asked on the long drive home from town in the evening traffic.

"The same," Mama said.

In the field below the village a thin coat of snow lay in the furrows between the cornstalks, and turning into Glendale we slowed. Old houses were gray at the backs of their lawns. The streetlamps came on. I thought, Grandfather Nye's death has begun.

"Lisa will be in at eight fifty-five in the morning," Daddy said. "If the Boston train is on time for a change."

When we were having drinks before dinner, Daddy put his hand on my shoulder and pulled back his head to look at me, but he didn't. "I'm glad you're home, my dear," he said. His mouth was enlarged and curved down the way it got after too much alcohol. His green eyes looked blurred and hurt.

"Oh, Daddy, I am too," I said.

He walked across the living room, his long thin body tilted slightly to the side. ("Erect but awkwardly," he used to say, and I always laughed.) His feet seemed slippery on the gold carpet. He went out to the kitchen to bring us more drinks.

"You know how a hospital upsets Morgan," Mama said. "Let alone seeing his father like this." In a minute she said, "I wish you wouldn't have to remember your grandfather this way, Vanessa."

"Mama, I want to go see him," I said.

"Wait until Daddy suggests it, though," she said.

Then we heard Eugenie's warm bronze voice booming out in the kitchen. She was talking to Daddy. I ran out to the kitchen. "Eugenie!" I hugged her. "It's wonderful to see you."

"You look fine, sweetheart, just fine," Eugenie said, her dark face shining. "That California sun is doin' you good."

Laelaps scratched on the kitchen door. "Well, here's the boss," Eugenie said. She went to the door, and in dashed Laelaps, bringing cold air on his fur.

"Good boy," I said, patting him. "Good boy."

"How's your grandfather today?" she asked when Daddy went out of the room.

"I don't know, Eugenie," I said.

"It's a hard time for your daddy," Eugenie said. "You be good to him now."

Just before dinner I went into the dining room. Daddy had turned on the little lights in the corner case that had come from Grandpa Nye's house in the spring, when Aunt Janice had moved him to their new house in Indian Hill. "Oh, Daddy, how nice," I said so he could hear me in the living room. In the dark room the velvet shelves looked like tiers of tiny stages where scarabs crawled, cats danced and posed and played on musical instruments side by side with bear teeth and Indian arrowheads. I lit the candles. The bronze bull gleamed in the dark over the corner case, and bits of gold light shone in the goblets on the table.

"The fatted calf," Mama said, beaming.

"Mama, you look beautiful," I said. In her face there was a luminous quality, a delicate sensual female look mixed with the first gentleness of age.

"I only wish . . ." Mama said, sighing, and breaking off as Daddy came into the room.

At dinner Daddy's head was lowered over his plate so his eyes seemed to be shut. "Morgan," Mama said, "I wish you would eat." He jerked his head up and looked at her.

Mama, I screamed inside me, leave him alone.

Aunt Aggie came over for dessert. "Vanesser, you look wonderful," she said. She smiled, shaking her head, her soft double chin. "Sister," she said, extending her hand to Mama, and I was home hearing again Aunt Aggie's nasal down-to-earth voice. When Daddy went to get the cognac, she said quietly, "Isabel, how is Morgan's father today?"

Then we heard the front door open and Charles, my favorite of all my cousins, called. I ran to greet him. "Cuz!" I laughed, and we hugged each other tightly.

"Cuz!" He smiled down at me, his dark face reddening. "It's good to have you home. You look great, sweetie," he said in his deep voice.

We stood together by the register talking. "How has Daddy been?" I asked him.

"Aunt Janice shouldn't have put Grandpa Nye in the hospital," Charles said. "It's been more than a month now, you know."

Aunt Aggie and Mama and Daddy came into the living room, bringing the coffee and cognac on a tray. "Move away from the register, children," Aunt Aggie shouted. "It's not healthy."

I sat on the couch by Aunt Aggie. Daddy and Charles stood by the fire. "Isn't she gorgeous?" Daddy said to Charles, and they looked across the room at me. I flushed with happiness.

Later I sat in my room, my old books around me, holding in what would make me cry: Mama and Daddy were so happy to have me home, and Daddy seemed thin and gray (in my mind when I was away his hair was dark). Mama smiled up at me, her eyes full of love (in my mind she was bigger than I, and her white-fleshed arms, her cold hands, her voice controlled me, pressed me down).

When I got into bed and turned out the light, I put my legs down where it felt like silk ice and drew them up again for warmth the way I used to as a child. I listened to the house's spaces, and I could almost hear the darkness flowing from room to room and up and down the stairs. I thought of the empty mirrors all over the house.

I remembered my terror in the nights long ago. Once I woke up and saw a man standing over by the mantelpiece. I slid down under the covers and tried not to breathe or make any sound, and I lay that way for hours—rigid, barely breathing. I thought he was Dillinger and if he knew I was there, he would kidnap me.

I used to dream I was in Grandmother Marston's house and I was alone. I was afraid and I began calling, "Mama. Mama." But no one was there. Then I saw the rooms were empty and there were no longer any windows. I wanted to get out. "Mama," I called. But no one was there. I couldn't get out. I went to the room that was the guest room. Like the other rooms it was light even though there were no windows. The walls were hard white, pink and blue wallpaper. The light was white and in the corner was a white bureau, so clean it shone. I was looking for something that was in the top right drawer and I tried to get there, but the floor of the room began to tilt so I couldn't get there. I was sliding back. I woke up terrified.

I thought, later, that in that dream I was looking for the pearl. The one Daddy found in his oyster stew one day when we had lunch at Grandmother Marston's. Lisa and I didn't want to eat ours and Daddy said whoever finished first would get the pearl. Lisa won the pearl. Then she lost it. I had the queer feeling I *made* her lose it somehow.

Late the next afternoon (December 23), Lisa and Amy—Lisa's little girl; she was two and a half—and Mama and I were having tea at Aunt Aggie's. Mama sent me home ahead of them to keep Daddy company if he had come home from the office.

He was out in the kitchen at the sink, his long back hunched around his glass. He tipped back his head and drank his scotch, then filled his glass with water and drank that. He set the glass on the counter and turned. His mouth was enlarged and curved down.

"How is Grandpa Nye?" I asked. "Did Aunt Janice call you?"

"Yes," he said. He clamped his mouth shut. "He's not going to get any better, my dear." He struggled with his lips when he spoke, and I remembered the time Mama went to be with Lisa when Amy was born, and I was in Michigan with Daddy, who was leaning against the beech tree out in back, his lips twitching with exasperation. "All I ask is to live long enough to bury Papa," he had said.

Now in the same voice he said, "You're off base, my dear. I love you, but you're off base. You've got to start thinking about what's important."

I stood there paralyzed.

"I don't see why you aren't going forward. We've given you a good education. You have the finest intellectual inheritance."

I saw him talking as if he were behind a pane of

glass. I wanted to step forward through the glass and smash his head. But I loved him. My father. Our skin was the same olive and in our skin was the same oil.

"I'm not going to live forever, my dear," he said.

"Listen, Daddy," I said, furious. "I'm doing what I can. I've had a lot of problems and troubles you don't know anything about."

"Oh, Vanessa," he said, "why don't you ever tell us anything? We want to know about you."

Just then Mama came into the kitchen. She looked at him and her arm jerked impatiently. "Morgan, shall I fix you some tomato juice?" she said.

"No, thank you," he said abruptly.

Mama went to the icebox, and as she got out the tomato juice in its plastic container, a little juice spilled on her wrist. Her body humped up, and she made a bloodcurdling sound, drawing breath through her teeth. Daddy swung around toward her. When he saw it was nothing, he was beside himself. "Isabel, you don't know how that made me feel. If you think I don't love you, you ought to know how that made me feel."

"I'm sorry," Mama said, not looking at him. She crossed the room in her heavy way, poured the tomato juice into a glass, got out some Trisquits, and put them on a plate. Then they left the room to go shower and dress. Mama was carrying the juice and the plate.

"Jesus, Lisa, sometimes I can't stand it here," I said to her when we converged in the dining room.

"Me either," Lisa said.

"Me either," Amy said.

"Amy," I said. I touched the soft top of her head.

"You'd think I'd be more detached with Amy and Stewart, but I'm not," Lisa said. Stewart was a doctor, a resident at Massachusetts General in Boston, and he had to be on duty over Christmas.

"It's going to be horrible at dinner," I said. "But fatted calf, cutie."

Upstairs in the bathroom Lisa and I combed our hair and put on lipstick. I looked at her lovely clear-featured face, her blue eyes, in the mirror.

"You have more bosom than me," she said.

"More bottom," I said mournfully.

"Well, Vanessa, it's not as bad as I used to think. They're meant to be sexy."

Mama came in, her eyes full of tears. "Sometimes I can't stand it any longer, and I'm never allowed to show how I feel," she said.

174

In a little while Mama and Lisa were out in the kitchen, talking. Daddy was reading *Time* in the study. Amy was drawing a picture in the hall at the foot of the stairs. "Watch me draw, Vanessa," she said. I sat down beside her. Her face still had its baby plumpness, and at the same time she had a look so delicate she seemed otherworldly. She drew a jaggedy line around and up and down. I saw the sweet flesh of her arm, her fierce will. When she finished, she gave it to me.

"Oh, it's very nice," I said.

"Vanessa," she said, "shut your eyes."

I did.

"Hold your nose."

I did.

She stood up and came over to peer. I watched her through my lashes. She put out her hand and lifted my eyelid, then the other; then she took my hand away from my nose. She stepped into my lap and hugged me. I put my arms around her. Fragrant child. I could feel her warm perfect back, her heart beating in her chest, I could feel her spirit inside her head.

"You know what we have to do?" I asked.

"What?"

"Set the table."

"Oh," she said.

It was dark in the dining room. As we went by the mantelpiece, I touched its smooth cold white surface and remembered how Daddy marked our heights with a pencil each year, and once suddenly I was as tall as the mantelpiece. It felt hard and tingly pressing on the top of my head and I kept going under it. I called Grandpa Nye to come see. I could see him still, standing in the doorway, tall and white-haired and stonelike as he was then.

Now I heard a train coming from down the valley. "Amy, do you want to see the train go by?" I lifted her onto a chair in the bay window and stood behind her. She stiffened as the train passed. The evening train to Detroit. I saw its lights sliding swiftly across her face.

Mama came in and turned on the light.

"Grandmama," Amy said, "I saw the train."

"Lisa," I said, "she's so beautiful."

Daddy stood at the door. "I want to go see Papa in the morning," he said. "Would you like to go?"

We said we would.

"We'll leave at exactly eleven," he said.

After supper, Lisa and Mama and I sat in the study and listened to Daddy make his way slowly up the stairs to bed. When he reached the top, Mama picked up her detective book and Lisa and I decided to take Laelaps for a walk.

Outside it was cold. There was a golden gray flower of altocumulus clouds in the south where the moon was. Laelaps tugged on his leash. The Farneys' Christmas tree was on. As we went down toward the tracks, we could hear a dog bark over the hill and another one answer. A train whistled in the next valley, and a big truck went by way up on the pike.

"Mama's just trying to *escape* with all those detective books," Lisa said.

"Ummh," I said.

"Remember in the war when she worked at the draft board?" Lisa said. "She used to sit there night after night, reading under that light with her legs apart, surrounded by smoke. She didn't budge until after midnight. I used to be so ashamed."

We climbed the mound to the tracks and walked along the switch. "Laelaps, do you want to see the cows?" I asked. He looked around and wagged his upright tail.

177

"It's good to have someone to talk to," Lisa said.

"Yes," I said.

"As Mama always said, marriage is no bed of roses."

"No, not for anyone, I guess."

"It's worth it, though."

"Yes," I said. "I know."

"Everyone loves Stewart at the hospital. They worship him. He doesn't really love me, that's what I have to face. Vanessa, he never shows me one bit of affection. He comes home and eats—he doesn't even notice his food. Then he goes and lies down. After Amy's asleep, he wakes up and comes to sit in the living room. If I want to talk, he picks up the paper right in the middle. And as for . . ."

"What?" I said tentatively.

"Well, never mind."

"Oh, Lisa," I said, full of the tension of wanting to say something and not being able.

"And Amy's afraid of him," she said in a while.

We turned off the tracks and started up Oak Road along the pasture. "I don't see the cows," she said.

"I didn't think of it before, but they're probably in bed," I said.

"I suppose so," she said sadly. Lisa loved cows.

Daddy used to be able to moo and make them come over to the fence for us. "I don't always feel this way," she said.

"I know," I said.

"It's so complex, Vanessa. Sometimes I can't stand it any longer. But. Well, once I was going to leave. I was really going to leave. And he said never leave him whatever I did. He cried. We both did."

We walked on, not talking, to the top of the hill where the Osage oranges grew. It was our favorite place to walk on Sunday afternoons when we were little, because when we reached the top we could bowl the Osage oranges down the hill and see whose went farthest and, best of all, whose rolled under a car to be squashed. In the dark we each found a cold one and threw it from the top of the hill and listened to it plop on the road. We laughed and then ran with Laelaps until we were out of breath. Below a few car lights were spinning through the winding village streets. There were pools of street-lamp glow and the darkness of houses and trees. The night was windless, and it felt as if a whirring sound were in the soft December earth, and in the naked trees were ghosts of whispers. It was as if these trees of southern Ohio held the voices of all my old knowing and the voices of older things I never knew. I wanted to go rub my face into the thick pasture grass, into the earth, to embrace the trees and eat their bark, to put my throat where the branch and trunk of a maple tree joined.

Away from here I was free of the love that made me want to cry all the time, but away from here I wasn't here where I belonged. Here slowly everything changed. I had to look to what was left of what I loved. I had to look at it more fiercely to make it larger than it was. Factories were filling the valley, and the air on still cloudy nights was filled with the rhythmic roar of the Wright plant making bombers all day, all night, but I could not think about the Wright plant, or about the place in that valley, but farther north, where they said atomic bombs were stored. It was beyond Mr. Northrop's woods and the Eliza house; it was in the next valley. I could not think about the fact that it took just three minutes to drive there in a car, and that from an airplane we and it were all the same.

Our house when we returned looked tall and pale in the moonglow. The light in Mama and Daddy's room was on, and then it went out. Mama was in bed.

I remembered once when I was out of college, returning from a walk with Daddy, we saw Mama go by the window in their room, framed and clear for an instant in the blue afternoon light. Daddy's arm shot up like a little boy's and waved to her, but she was gone from the window and never saw.

"Let's drink some of Grandpa Nye's wine," Lisa said when we hung up our coats. We went out to the kitchen. I got one of his bottles from the closet, and as I held it up to the light, I remembered the way Grandpa Nye held a bottle to the light in the cold room in his cellar where Lisa and I accompanied him each time we went to dinner there. Before dinner we would go into the library and stand behind the high back of Grandpa Nye's green velvet chair and wait until he remembered and said, "Lisa and Vanessa, how would you like to go down to the cellar with me for a moment?"

We went down the dark back hall and down the steep stairs. In the cellar it was as still and peaceful as an underwater world. The whitewashed walls were thick and bumpy. On a deep ledge opposite the furnace, evening sun came in through greenhouse glass and sifted through the leaves of plants that had been

growing since long before our time. Flecks of sunlight swirled in the masses of green weeds in the
guppy bowls; guppies darted here and there.

Grandpa Nye moved slowly, and in the clear abstract concentration of his eyes we sensed the wild
Grandpa Nye who yearly in autumn climbed high
trees along the banks of the Ohio for wild grapes for
his wine.

In autumn Grandpa Nye smelled of the grape and
there was purple in the lines of his old fingers; and
in winter at his dinner table he drank toasts in frail
honey-colored goblets and was joyous.

In autumn Grandpa Nye worked out in back pick-
ing grapes from their bunches. The sky was pale; yellow leaves fell through the air. Grandpa Nye put the
grapes in huge crockery vats, covered them with
cheesecloth, and listened for the day when it would
be time to siphon the new wine from the vats, to
press the skins, and transfer the wine to oaken barrels in the cellar. In autumn Grandpa Nye in his old
purple- and bark-stained clothes spread out his arms
and said, "'Season of mists and mellow fruitfulness!
Close bosom-friend of the maturing sun.'"

And in winter he tended his cellar. When Lisa and
I went down with him, he walked through the fur-

nace room and into the cold room where wine in bottles lay on racks from the floor to the ceiling. Here he would select two bottles—one for dinner, and one for Daddy to take home. "Vanessa," he said, holding one up to the light, "how do you think this one will do for your father?" There was dust on his sleeve and a cylindrical well of light in the red wine.

"I think that's a perfect one, Grandpa Nye," I said.

He gave us each a bottle to carry and we went into the dark room on the far side of the furnace where the wine fermented in barrels. In there it smelled of earth and oak wood. Grandpa Nye lit matches to check the keg tubes for bubbles, and his face was lit in the dark like a face appearing in a warm dream. When the gas stopped bubbling, Grandpa Nye would transfer the wine to sealed barrels, where as the grapes flowered in spring it would undergo its slighter third fermentation, its fourth as the new grapes ripened in autumn. And on a bright day after that Grandpa Nye would bottle the wine on the long table in the room with the sun and the plants.

With a final match Grandpa Nye checked the thermometer, and sometimes on the stairs as we started back he turned and spoke. "Wine prolongs life," he said. Once he turned and bellowed out like a line of poetry, "'The grape, boys, the grape!'" In the digni-fied voice that he used to discuss our ancestors, he said, "Lisa and Vanessa, a branch of the DeGolyer family owns to this day some of the finest vineyards of the Bordeaux country." Another time, without turning, he said absently to himself, "'Drink deep ere you depart.'" And I saw his head nod slightly as old men's heads do.

Now in our kitchen as I set the bottle of his wine down on the table, I could hear his feet, heavy and slow, as they were in later years, scraping across the cellar floor. Lisa sat staring dreamily into the wine.

Charles told me that when it got close to the time to move, Grandpa Nye always got up when Daddy or he came to visit and met them at the door. "Charles," he would say, "what is being done about my wine?" "Morgan," he said, "what is being done about my wine?" They didn't know how to answer.

They went into the library and tried to speak with the old focus, to sound the way they had always sounded.

"Papa," Daddy said, "we saw the first robin to-day." Grandpa Nye sat still, his collar crooked, his bow tie askew. His eyes in his veiny face were febrile and blue. "Papa," Daddy said, "did you see the article on Afghanistan in the new *Geographic*?"

Grandpa Nye's eyes were abstract as though straining for release, and when they had been there just a few minutes, he would get abruptly up from his chair and start across the entrance hall.

"Nate, where are you going?" Aunt Janice called. As she went to bring him back, the family whispered, "We ought to go, he's tired today."

Charles said to me, "Once she had bought that house and started the remodeling, everything was already done."

Daddy said, "Papa started going downhill rapidly some time after you left last Christmas."

Now I got the corkscrew and went into the dining room for glasses. In the cabinet I found the honey-colored goblets from Grandpa Nye's house. I carried them gingerly, one in each hand.

"These glasses," I said to Lisa. When they were set on the white tablecloth at Grandpa Nye's house, their fragile surfaces, like bubble walls, caught the reds, the greens, the golds of the mosaic lampshade that hung down over the center of the table.

Lisa opened the bottle and poured the wine. I lifted the goblet. The wine shriveled the flesh in my mouth.

"Oh, Vanessa, it's bitter," Lisa cried.

"It's gone bad," I said.

"She could have put in an elevator," Lisa said after a while.

"I think he hoped he'd die before he had to move," I said.

"Think how old he is, Vanessa," Lisa said. He was ninety-two.

"Vanessa," she said in a minute, "do you think she would have done it if the house hadn't been left to his boys?"

"The house was originally in Grandmother Nye's name," I said. "That's why it was left to them when she died, did you know that?" In a minute I said, "We could open another bottle, but probably we should save it. Charles told me that when they were cleaning out the house they used to drink a bottle of wine each time they went and take home a bottle or two, but then one Saturday when they got there the wine was gone. She must have hired a truck to have it taken away. No one knew where it went."

When Lisa and I went up to bed, we went in to cover Amy and see her sleeping.

"I love her when I see her that way," Lisa said back in my room. "At home she drives me nuts half the time, Vanessa. She won't let me alone. She does things on purpose to make me mad."

"What does she do?" I said.

"Oh, she goes outside and does doo-doo in her pants just because she knows it makes me mad. And Stewart's no help. But here she's got all of you to . . . I can appreciate her more. But you don't know . . ."

"What?"

"You don't know what she's really like," Lisa said with fury in her voice.

We turned out the light and pulled the covers up to our chins. Branch shadows made by the street lamp on the corner emerged in the white patch of light on my door. "Remember when we thought they were the movies?" I said, remembering the wonder of waking and seeing the movies there on my door in the middle of the night—branches, witches, animals, magic, all silent and mysterious. I ran to get Lisa and bring her to my room and then side by side on the cold floor we sat spellbound, watching little things flicker and run along the branches.

Lisa didn't answer. She was asleep. I got up and went out of the room and downstairs. I walked in the dark through the living room and opened the front door and breathed in the quiet of the village, of the street lamp shining at the corner, and remembered being in the dark of the church long ago before the Christmas pageant. We were singing "O Little Town of Bethlehem." The church was warm and on everything visible lay the sheen of candlelight. I was very small and there was a burning in my head and my chest because in the moment we sang "Yet in thy dark streets shineth the everlasting light," I saw Bethlehem far away under the heaven. I saw its wet streets with lights shining in them on a rainy night in winter; I saw it so clearly I could have reached out and touched the sliver of light in a puddle and made it shake.

December 24: Eugenie came in as Lisa and I were lazily finishing breakfast in the kitchen. Mama and Amy were sitting with us. Daddy had laid out his office work on the dining-room table, and he was in there working.

"Vanessa," Eugenie boomed, "you could write a book about what we come across cleaning out your grandfather's house."

"The filth!" Mama said, drawing breath through her teeth.

188

THE DEAD OF THE HOUSE

"The dirt in that house," Eugenie said.

"It even gave young Charles the heebie-jeebies," Mama said.

"And Miss Janice always going around looking so clean and neat," Eugenie said in the mincing voice she used to show disapproval.

Mama said, "We found a bag of socks in an upstairs closet that Daddy sent home from Princeton to be washed—in *1922*!"

"Yes," Eugenie said. "That house about sent me into retirement for good." Eugenie was always threatening to retire. "Work makes for too much income tax," she always said.

"We found *sixteen* high silk hats in the attic," Mama said. "Mr. Nye used to wear them in the days when he lectured, and later on business trips. He was always leaving one behind, so he had to buy another, and then the one left behind would be returned."

I wished I could have heard him lecturing. I had heard him speak in public only once—on a raw October day in 1952 when he was eighty-nine, a week after the first of his heart attacks. He was very ill, but he would not be kept from coming, as he had long dreamed, to lay the cornerstone of the new Cincinnati Library. He had been a member of the Library

Board for more than fifty years, and its chairman for more than twenty-five. He had been a member of the Library Board for so long that when in court once, testifying in behalf of the character of a well-known Cincinnati bookseller accused of having knowingly bought books stolen from the Library of Congress, he was asked by the lawyer from Washington how long had he been a member of the Library Board, the judge interposed and said, "It is a matter of public knowledge that Mr. Nye has been a member of the Board of Trustees of the Public Library of Cincinnati as long as the memory of man doth have it." And in all that time he had worked trying to get a new main library for the city. In an editorial, the *Enquirer* called him Mr. Library and told how as far back as the turn of the century he had gone personally to Pittsburgh to see Andrew Carnegie, hoping to get money for the new main library. He had come back, instead, with the funds for eight branch libraries. It told how Grandpa Nye had once, in the Depression, borrowed $180,000.00 in his own name to keep the doors of the library open, and how he had, through the years, worked tirelessly for the passage of bond issues which failed six times before at last the money for the new building was voted. And then, as his dream was about to come true, he was struck down by illness. Or so it was thought. Certainly no one expected to see him. But at two o'clock, just as the ceremonies were about to begin, a black limousine drew up to the curb, and the chauffeur helped Grandpa Nye to the sidewalk and across it. He looked very white and frail. The first snowflakes were flying in the bitter wind. But still, he spread out his arms and spoke in his grand old style. His voice was so weak it was lost at moments amid the sounds of the city, but I heard him speak of the wilderness, of the trees of great magnitude that once grew where we now stood; he spoke of how few foresaw in those days, as did General Richard Butler in 1795, that this would some day be the abode of thousands, that cities would grow up to rival Rome and Athens. He spoke of that proud moment in our city's early history in May of 1825 when General Lafayette, on his triumphal tour, visited Cincinnati. He was rowed across the river from Kentucky on a barge, beautifully decorated; the rowers were the foremost young men of the city. General Lafayette was welcomed to Ohio by Governor Morrow and borne in a carriage to a platform in front of the hotel at the foot of Broadway where he was addressed by General William Henry Harrison, the best-known man in the Northwest and Cincinnati's most distinguished citizen. In his brief felicitous oration General Harrison said, among other things, "There is no deception, General, in the appearances of prosperity which are before you. This flourishing city has not been built, like the proud capital on the frozen Neva, by the command of a despot, directing the labor of obedient millions. It has been reared by the hands of free men . . ."

Grandpa Nye spoke of the library as the snowfall thickened. And then he stepped down and took the trowel in hand and laid the cornerstone of the new Cincinnati library, while opposite him in Garfield Park rode the bronze horseman, William Henry Harrison.

Speaking of the occasion later, Daddy said, "It was snowing. Nathaniel J. Nye, bareheaded, made a speech. It was his last speech in public."

Now in our kitchen Mama said gaily, "Eugenie, we've got work to do. There will be eleven for dinner." Mama counted on her fingers. "The four of us, young Charles and Miss Edie, Big Charles and Mrs. Nye, Mr. Edward . . ." Uncle Charles and Aunt Melissa were coming in from Washington to stay with Charles and Edie. Uncle Edward was coming down from Toronto to be near Grandpa Nye. His children all were married and living in the East. Aunt Kate, his wife, had died three years ago. "He can't seem to get over it," Daddy told me. "And he's exceedingly worried about remarrying. Exceedingly worried. He's afraid he'll marry someone who will turn out to be like Janice."

"And Miss Aggie," Mama continued. "And Miss Janice. Eleven, that's right."

Daddy came into the kitchen. "Good morning, Eugenie," Daddy said. You could always tell through Daddy's perfect manners who he loved, and he loved Eugenie. He pulled his gold watch out of his vest pocket. His hand shook. "I want to leave in exactly ten minutes," he said to us.

Grandpa Nye's room was white with daylight. He was lying in bed propped up on pillows, wearing a white hospital gown. He was staring straight before him, and he didn't turn his head when Aunt Janice came to kiss us. She was lovely and pale in a soft blue suit. She smelled of her gardenia perfume.

Grandpa Nye's blue eyes were fixed. They looked empty and wild, and at the same time terror-stricken

193

His hair was long; it was flying out from his head. His forehead was so pale it shone. His mouth hung open and his face was covered with prickles of white hair. But he knew we were there. He tried to get hold of the sheet and pull it to cover himself. He couldn't seem to grab hold of it. I saw his naked gray thigh.

"All right, dear," Aunt Janice said, and she did it for him.

Then he lifted his hand, which was enormous and blue-veined, hanging at the end of his thin arm. He moved his hand slowly across himself and Daddy walked down by the side of the bed and took it.

"Hello, Papa," Daddy said.

"See!" Aunt Janice squealed. "He's still strong as an ox." She giggled excitedly.

"Hello, Grandpa Nye," I said. His hand was strong and smooth like the hand of a statue. I was sure he knew us.

"Hello, Grandpa Nye," Lisa said.

Daddy sat on the edge of the bed. His washed hands trembled and he folded them together. "Papa . . ." he said. "Papa . . ." Daddy couldn't think what to say.

Lisa and I were standing at the foot of the bed. There were mounds of flowers on the bureau behind us, and they were dying; the water in the vases was turning brown. Grandpa Nye's purplish coated mouth was hanging open and he seemed to be looking through us, beyond us into the dying flower petals.

Lisa said, "Stewart sent you his regards, Grandpa Nye." Then she said, "Amy knew we were coming to see her great-grandfather this morning."

I wouldn't have known him, but I could see his hooked DeGolyer nose and the dark mole on the side of his temple. And under his hospital gown on his thin old chest there were still, I knew, the scars of his tattoo, the L F B M, which stood for Lively Five of the Blue Miami, and the skull and crossbones.

Grandpa Nye tried to speak. His voice was caught down in his chest. It sounded like a car engine starting up over and over and failing. His mouth worked. Then he was quiet.

"What, dear?" Aunt Janice said.

The droning and grinding started up in his chest again. Finally I could hear that he was saying, "I'm a sick man." He was saying it over and over, trying to make us understand.

"I'm a sick man," Janice repeated as if she'd just made out the talk of a baby. "Some days he speaks quite clearly," she said. "He must have had another little stroke in the night."

"Papa," Daddy said, "Vanessa arrived on Tuesday from California. Lisa and Amy got in Wednesday morning. The Boston train was on time for a change."

Grandpa Nye stared wildly.

Janice began talking of Calvin's last illness and his death in her high insistent voice. "He died a week ago today," she said. "Well, Dr. Niemeyer said, 'Mrs. Nye, there is nothing more I can do for your little dog.' 'Yes,' I said, 'there is one thing more you can do, Dr. Niemeyer.'" Aunt Janice paused and looked slowly and significantly into all our eyes. "Calvin didn't suffer at the end," she said wagging her finger, her polished pink fingernail. "I took him home in his own little suitcase and kept him in the pantry overnight. The next morning early I got the shovel out of the garage and went out in back to start digging. I'd hardly gotten a spadeful out of the earth when young Neil Carlson came over. 'Let me help you, Mrs. Nye,' he said. 'I'm so sorry to hear that Calvin passed on.' 'My dear boy,' I said, 'you *can* help me.'" She made a kissing sound and paused significantly. "You can't imagine how hard that young boy worked. After a while I said, 'Neil, dear, you mustn't spend your whole day when you are on vacation over here helping me.' 'Mrs. Nye,' he said, 'you wouldn't want Calvin to be disturbed, would you?' Isn't that sweet?" she said with one of her giggles. And then emphatically, insistently, "I buried him deep. I buried him deep."

Grandpa Nye's mouth worked. His voice down in his chest started up. Finally I heard that he was saying "Oh, my."

Aunt Janice repeated, "Oh, my."

Daddy stood up and went to the window. "The river is beginning to rise, Papa," he said. "There were heavy rains in West Virginia and Pennsylvania last week."

A nurse looked in at the door. "How are we this morning?" she said.

Grandpa Nye twisted under his sheet.

"We're not so well today," Janice said. "I think we had another little stroke in the night."

Daddy said, "Well, Papa, it has been very nice to see you. We'll come again tomorrow."

We all took his hand, and as we were leaving his room I looked back. He was sitting up and watching us go.

Aunt Janice came down with us. When we reached the lobby, she drew Daddy aside. She clutched his arm and looked around. "Morgan, I can't move him out of here," she said. "I simply can't. Won't you do something? Couldn't you call Dr. Schwarz? There would have to be two nurses at least. They eat like horses, you know, so even if—"

"Excuse me, Janice," he said, "I have to get out of here." He said he would call Dr. Schwarz.

When we got in the car, Daddy got his old Princeton flask out of the glove compartment. "Excuse me," he said. "I can't take it." He took a drink. Then he took another. The Hudson Bay scotch was fragrant and a brown drop of it trickled down his chin.

"Daddy, why can't he go home?" I said.

Daddy looked at me with a furious look. "Vanessa, you don't know what you're talking about," he said.

At lunch when Daddy went out to feed the birds, Mama said, "He's more comfortable in there. Remember, girls, how much she's done for him, too."

"I wouldn't have known him," Lisa said.

Mama said, "Everyone is coming at seven-thirty, so we ought to be dressed and ready by six-thirty for hanging Amy's stocking."

————

After lunch Daddy and I took a walk with Laelaps. Daddy wore his felt hat, his kid gloves. He carried his polished cane and we walked rapidly, for he made a point of maintaining at all times exactly the pace he maintained daily on Fourth Street when he walked from his office to the University Club for lunch and back.

"Papa didn't always handle things correctly," Daddy said.

"What do you mean?" I said.

"In business," Daddy said. "Papa was a fall guy for anyone who wanted money. People *warned* Papa that blankety-blank-blank lawyer was crooked. "People *warned* Papa. I heard them myself."

Daddy was talking about the man who was responsible for the ruin of the Morgan Burke Company.

"There were always great ups and downs in that business," Daddy told me once. "In the panic of 1907 Papa called up Andrew Carnegie in Pittsburgh—it was Papa's first long-distance call—and they made a deal that enriched them both. Papa told Mr. Carnegie that he had on hand such and such a number of tons of pig iron at such and such the ton. And Mr. Carne-

199

gie said he'd buy all the pig iron Papa had on hand, and all Papa could get hold of at the figure he had named. Papa was able to purchase vast amounts of pig iron all over the South at panic prices and sell it thus to Mr. Carnegie for a considerable profit. By spring, Mr. Carnegie had all the iron in this part of the country."

"What exactly did that lawyer do, Daddy?" I wanted to know. "I've never understood."

"He was a crooked shyster lawyer," Daddy said. "The plan was for the Morgan Burke Company to ship iron and coal to a Europe devastated by war, and to import rich manganese ore which had been seen piled and unused at docks on the Black Sea by your Uncle Charles and Uncle Edward when they were there after the war. The ships were to be leased out of Lebanon or Greece. That's a common practice even now. But money was to be invested in a company to conduct the operation. Stock had to be issued. That crooked shyster lawyer had the Morgan Burke Company issue itself a million dollars' worth of stock. Actually, no money was invested at all. Then he led other companies to invest considerable sums in the belief that there was already a good deal of capital in the company. But there wasn't, and the whole thing blew up.

"That was in May of 1924," Daddy said. "Your mother and I were newly married. We were living in Ashland then. I was working as a time-study man for Armco. I'd already worked at blast furnaces in Hamilton and Ironton, and in an iron-ore mine in Alabama, and I'd worked in the coal mines in Hazard. I had no inkling it was coming. No *inkling*." Daddy's lips began to twitch with anger. "I woke up one morning in Ashland and the headlines were two inches high: MORGAN BURKE CO. FAILS. The Morgan Burke Company was sued for all it was worth. We were all ruined. We were wiped out. And that blankety-blank-blank lawyer went to California and shot himself. Papa brought suit, you know, and that man's secretary told the truth under oath in court. His widow was left with more money than any of us will ever have. You went to dancing school with one of his grandchildren."

"Who?" I asked.

"Never mind, I'm not going to tell you," he said.

"Papa was a millionaire at one time," Daddy said,

"and he liked to live in an expansive fashion. He was a different man from that day."

In a minute Daddy said, "If ever a man was 'insecure,' it was I when you children were little. If I had known what was coming, I would have . . ."

"What?"

"I would have become a teacher," he said. "Papa could be tough. In the summer after I graduated from Princeton he bought me a one-way ticket to Ironton and he gave me eighty cents. That's all I had to my name."

When we got back to the house, I asked Daddy if I could take one of the cars. I wanted to drive over and look at Grandpa Nye's house.

"I'd rather you wouldn't," Daddy said. "I can't drive by the place any more. It makes me too unhappy. We can't sell it for much, you know. It was in terrible condition."

"I'd just like to see it again," I said.

"All right, my dear, take your mother's car," he said "The telephone is still connected. I wanted to keep it connected until we sell the house. Just one of my usual half-baked ideas. We hired old Green Collins to wash the windows, and he didn't stay to finish the job. He said there was a 'hant' in the house, and he wouldn't go back."

It took about twenty-five minutes to get to Grandpa Nye's. I drove down Salt Lick Avenue the way we always did, past the old gray stone mansions and the newer houses. His house looked immense and gentle—the old red bricks, the white columned porch, the high gambrel roof, the attic dormers. But the windows were empty and wild. I went up the walk past the gingko tree and the place where the petrified log used to be, and up the steps onto the porch. I could see through the glass door and into the empty house and out the dining-room windows to the woods beyond. I tried the door. It was locked. I went around to the side and up on the screen porch, lifted the window to the library and climbed in. For an instant I smelled the musky fragrance of old leather books, old pages, dust, polished wood, and Grandpa Nye's cigar, and I saw the library as it was last Christmas when I came to say good-bye to Grandpa Nye before I went back to California.

He was sitting in his green velvet chair at his desk, reading Coleridge's *Table Talk*. He motioned for me to sit down, and read aloud the passage he was reading as I came in. His hoarse old voice was thinner. "'Tenth July, 1834,'" he read. "'I am dying, but without expectation of a speedy release. Is it not strange that very recently bygone images and scenes of early life have stolen into my mind like breezes blown from the Spice Islands of Youth and Hope, those twin realities of this phantom world.'" Grandpa Nye marked his place and closed the book. "This morning as clearly as if it were yesterday," he said, "I remembered my Grandmother Nye buying me a little brown sugar man in the marketplace in Montreal. Then I remembered that when I was four or five my Grandfather Nye, for whom I was named, came to Brockville, where my father was principal of the grammar school, and took me to Montreal for a visit with him. We went on the old Grand Trunk Railway, and even now I remember the huge flaring smoke-stack of the wood-burning locomotive. The train ran into a snowdrift and we were stalled on the track. I can remember as if it were yesterday my grandfather's distress for fear I should go hungry. So he put on his greatcoat and left me in the charge of some kindly people on the train and walked off across the snowy fields to a distant farmhouse to procure food. I glued my face to the frosty pane and kept my eyes on him as long as he was in sight. At last, to my inexpressible relief he reappeared, bringing a basket in which were apples, cookies, bread, and butter." Grandpa Nye paused and he offered me a cigar.

"Oh, thank you, Grandpa Nye," I said. I puffed a great cloud of smoke.

"You take after your pirate ancestor on your Grandmother Nye's side of the family," he said with resignation. Then he said, slowly, as if it had just come back to his mind, "Do you know, Vanessa, last night I dreamed I saw my mother and father. They were as they were when I first knew them. They were young and handsome and well-to-do. They were in a room with many people dancing. Then my father was older. He was walking away, reading a book. He was killed, you know, by a train, while he was reading *Tess of the D'Urbervilles*."

He puffed on his cigar. His old mouth chewed. The light from the green lamp fell on his long, gentle face, and the leathery folds of his throat. His collar was crooked and his bow tie a bit askew. "My father and his father were readers," he said. "They were not woodsmen. But my Grandfather DeGolyer's people had been pioneers. In the next generation they were people of culture. They were preachers and teachers. They had imagination and enterprise. Yet all the DeGolyer men I knew had a pronounced out-of-doors streak in them. They were woodsmen. My Grandfather DeGolyer was a Baptist minister, but he had left his pulpit with a scheme for making money catching lake fish when he met his death. . . . As for me, I was never so happy as when I was in the north-land canoeing through the wilderness with my boys and their friends and Alfred, my Indian guide. In the city when I was younger, my days were restless and my nights of sleep were troubled; the long winter was tedious, and it was with great joy that I used to greet the wilderness again each summer. For me it held a healing balm."

His mind wandered off a moment. I saw his mouth sag. I remembered a poem he wrote in *Cedar and Spruce*, which I memorized when I was fifteen and I used to wait miserably through the winter to be back in Michigan, running through the woods, running up the beach again into the wind. Grandpa Nye wrote,

> Awake I dream and I behold
> Far rivers rushing wild and free

206

Flowing through forests dark and old
To meet the everlasting sea.

Amid the city's smoke and grime,
All wide-awake this dream I dream
Of far-off woods in summer time,
And silent lake and silver stream.

He said, "One day on the Albany River—in 1923,
I think it was—we saw a white man being paddled by
two Indians. At the time that was not for me, but I remember thinking then that when I would be very old
and no longer able to paddle a canoe in rapids or over
a portage, I would not object to being borne through
the wilderness that way on a flowery bed of ease. So
would I like to go now back through the forest to a
lake so lovely its memory still haunts me. It had
many islands, and its Indian name meant Lake of Everlasting Waters. I would like to return to it once
more and take it in my arms or let its waters enfold
me."

Grandpa Nye got up from his chair with difficulty
and walked slowly from the room, his feet shuffling
across the Oriental rug. I went down to the end of the
long library and looked out into the woods. When

he came back, he was carrying a silver tray with a pitcher and three cocktail glasses and a plate of crackers. "It's five o'clock," he said. "I never take a drink before five. Would you like a martini, Vanessa? Your Aunt Janice should be home any minute."

We sipped our martinis. "Do you know, Grandpa Nye," I said, "I used to think your woods were magic. When I was in school and I read *Dear Brutus* I loved it so I became enchanted. And I imagined your woods were like that. I thought they existed only there beyond your stone wall and that the only way to go into them was to go through your library and the dining room and the kitchen and out the back door and down by the woodpile and over the stile. I thought that if I did go into your woods, I would go back into the past and I'd never be able to come out again."

He smiled. "Of course there is something about trees and time," he said. "When I was a boy, our house on College Hill was on the old Gray Road, and I often walked eastward on that road, crossed the deep valley just before Spring Grove Cemetery was reached, to climb on the farther hilltop the biggest tree I have ever seen in Ohio. I worshiped that tree. It filled me with awesome admiration. I would visit it and try to think how long it had stood, how many generations of men it had known. Some years after I was married, I came that way and found the tree had gone. I felt a great pang of sorrow. And I never go into my woods now without in my mind going back in time. Sometimes I feel again the heated joy of afternoons when we boys—the Lively Five of the Blue Miami—roamed those woods, imagining we were the Indians before us. There was never a more lovely woodland stream than Bloody Run with its giant sycamores, its groves of beech, its clear waters. Sometimes I think of your father when he was a little shaver of four or five setting solemnly off on an expedition in search of arrowheads. . . . How is your father, Vanessa?"

"Oh, I don't know," I said. He heard the distress in my voice.

"He drinks too much these days," Grandpa Nye said. "But he'll get over it. Those are difficult years for a man." Daddy was fifty-three.

"Sometimes when I go into my woods I go back in my mind to the year 1791, when William Henry Harrison first came down the Ohio to assume his post at Fort Washington. I imagine the forest as it was then, when this country was all forest and the Ohio

209

shore was known as the Indian shore. If an ark drew too close, it was likely to be met with a volley of rifle fire from the Indians lurking in the trees by the river. This region was known in those days as the Miami Slaughter House."

I laughed.

"Bloody Run was so named because on it two of Wayne's soldiers were killed by Indians. A party of four had stopped their horses to drink from its limpid water when the Indians from ambush fired upon them."

Just then Aunt Janice came in. She'd been out in Indian Hill at the house, she said, and she had some new pictures of the remodeling that I hadn't seen. She got out her photograph album and opened it. "Look," she said, "isn't it going to be darling!" She pointed. "This is the breakfast nook. Isn't it sweet? Nate's desk will go here. These will be built-in shelves. Oh, I'm simply thrilled with it! Calvin's going to love his new home, aren't you, dear?" she said, bending down and lifting him up onto Grandpa Nye's lap. "Poor thing can't jump up any more," she said. "I'm afraid your grandfather is tired today, dear," she said.

I stood up and went over to the wide fireplace to

warm myself for a moment. I looked up at the painting—men in lederhosen, smoking pipes by a moun-
tain hut in the Tyrol—that was laid into the dark
mahogany paneling above the high mantelpiece. I
wondered what would happen to the painting when
they moved.

"I'm going to give you that painting, Vanessa,"
Aunt Janice said, "if you ever get married."

Grandpa Nye put Calvin down on the floor and
stood up. Together we went slowly to the door. "I
wish you would stay home, Vanessa," he said when I
kissed him and started to leave. He took my hand as
if he were going to tell me something more, but he
didn't

"Good-bye, Grandpa Nye," I said.

"Good-bye Vanessa," he said.

How clear he seemed then, I thought. But as it
came close to the time to move, his worries must
have grown to the point where he became helpless in
his anxiety. And the old anguish, the griefs, which
had been quiet these last years—they, too, must have
returned.

I imagined how when the movers came to pack
and the paintings were down off the walls, the books
out of the shelves, the dust swirling in the tunnels

211

of silver light slanting in from the windows, and the fireplace was cold, littered high with papers, Grandpa Nye sat alone in the library; and as he read he absently touched the books piled on his desk, his paper cutters, his paperweights, the bronze snake, the stems of his pipes, his pens, his pencils, and then, restless, he would get up and start across the hall, thinking it was already long past the time to transfer the wine to the sealed barrels; no one had checked the keg tubes to see—was it last autumn or the autumn before he had last felt the grapes in his fingers? It didn't matter, he thought, it didn't matter at all if it was too late. The point was to go down there and do it, work at it, and the noise of Janice directing the movers would turn down there into age-old sounds of wine fermenting, guppies nibbling, plants growing. And it wouldn't matter if he got tired. He'd sit down and the dust would fall on his hands and he'd put his head back to rest on the floor of his earth and the flecks of sun in the guppy bowls would settle gold into his eyes, and before the dark would come on, the rooms of his house would stand over him, clear, and warmly lit, and filled with happy people. And he'd see upstairs in their bedroom in the half-dark Laura—Laura lovely and slender as she was in the early days of their marriage. What was it that went wrong, he wondered. What had he failed to do?

"Keep Nate away from me," Laura screamed. "Keep him away." In the night when he was gone, she had heard voices in the attic. Spies in league with Margaret, their Bavarian cook, plotting to poison her, she thought.

"Go up and shoot them, they're talking about me," Laura screamed. "Go up and shoot them!" Morgan and Edward had gone up to the attic with the gun. Morgan still a boy. Charles was in Brussels then. And Joab? Poor Joab. Why had he been so hard on Joab? And such a giant die so young? Up in the attic Edward fired the shots. What was it he had failed to understand? The doctors said that Laura needed rest. Rest and solitude. He remembered how when she had been gone about a month, he went to the sanitarium to take her to Edward's wedding. She was dressed in blue; she was handsome and lovely as a girl of sixteen. The rest had done her good, he had thought then. It broke his heart to have to take her back to the sanitarium. But she said that she would not come home. She said their house was a house of sorrows. And the years he waited, the years he still hoped she would get well, she continued to say, *No, Never*, she would not come home, *Ever*.

So in age the torment tore at him again, I thought, and as he reached the door to the cellar stairs, he heard, "Nate!" Janice's voice broke like a white plate shattering in his mind. "Nate!" she said. She caught him by the sleeve. "Where are you going?"

Slowly, for her question had to reach him through the rooms of voices in his head, he answered, "I want to see about my wine."

"You know you can't go down there," she said. "Come back and sit down, dear."

He let himself be led back to his chair in the library. He took up and started reading where he had left off Boswell's *Journal of a Tour to the Hebrides*.

Now the gray light hung like ghosts at the windows, and I heard the whispered ends of my steps echoing as I crossed the hall and went out the front door. It smelled as if it were going to snow. I breathed in the fresh odor of the air and looked gratefully up at the black clouds sailing in from the north in low, soft masses.

I drove home the back way over the Wright plant highway and then across the bed of the old Miami and Erie Canal and up the hill by the Eliza house. I could remember Mama, long ago, slowing the car and saying, "Children, this is the Eliza house. This is where Eliza hid after she crossed the river on the ice." And I thought Eliza was still in there. I thought I'd come there alone some sunny day on my tricycle and wait quietly in the garden. Then after a while Eliza would come out and play with me. She was a little colored girl who was a slave, but now she was free.

When, at six-thirty, we came downstairs, Daddy had lighted the coal fire in the grate. The lamps were on and soft, the curtains drawn, and just as we came into the living room Daddy lighted the tree. And there it was on the night before Christmas, the branches reaching out and up, and in the spaces between there seemed to be a spirit caught. The branches were wound round and hung with lights and angel's hair and candy canes and colored balls, which were like myriad mirrors reflecting tiny living rooms and the tiny, funny faces of us as we drew close. Amy was soft-footed and enchanted, looking up.

Mama said, "Oh, Vanessa, I remember when you saw your first Christmas tree. You were just a year old and we took you up to Mother's. You came in, walking your little go-cart. When you saw the tree, you stopped and put your hands up—like this. 'Ahhh!' You said, 'Ahhh.'" Mama's eyes were shining.

I looked at Mama, a lump in my throat. She had felt so tenderly toward me, and I had never known it.

Lisa got the stockings and *The Night Before Christmas* from their box. She showed Amy how to hang her stocking by the chimney with care. It was Lisa's old one, which was pink-and-blue flannel, with bells around the top and on the toe.

"Santa Claus will come in the night and fill your stocking," Mama said.

"Remember once you woke us, Mama," I said, "because Santa Claus was going by in his sleigh."

"And we *heard* his bells," Lisa said.

"But when we got to the window and looked out in the snowy street, his sleigh was gone," I said.

"He had turned the corner down at St. Clair and gone on over to the village," Lisa said.

"The weatherman predicts snow for tonight," Daddy said.

Mama read in her glowing, sentimental reading voice. Amy sat with her legs straight out before her,

216

looking up at her grandmother, who, when she was two, could recite *The Night Before Christmas* from beginning to end by heart.

At the end, Lisa and I said with Mama, "'Merry Christmas to all, and to all a good night.'"

Daddy pulled out his watch. "Well, they should be here in another fifteen minutes," he said.

"Lisa, play *Joy to the World*," Mama said. It was Daddy's favorite and he often sang just that line— "Joy to the world"—no matter what the season.

Lisa went into the hall and played. Daddy tipped back his head, rapt and happy, humming. Mama said radiantly, "She has the touch, she *still* has the touch." Just then the doorbell rang and Laelaps came racing through the living room, barking at the top of his lungs. "I *wish* she wouldn't always ring the bell," Mama said.

Through the glass in the door I saw Aunt Janice's face, pale like the moon, in the porch light. Everyone came in more or less at once except for Charles, who had stopped to see Grandpa Nye on his way home from the office, Edie said, and would be along in another few minutes.

"It's cold as Greenland out tonight," Aunt Aggie shouted. "It's going to snow, they say."

"Oh, Edie, you're great with child," Lisa said, touching her high stomach. Edie laughed, and she lifted her lovely white throat and kissed Daddy. "Uncle Morgan," she said.

The room filled with our voices. I hugged Uncle Charles and kissed his mustache. "Oh, Uncle Charles, I'm so glad to see you," I said, the gladness rushing warmly through my blood.

A smile came into his sad green eyes. "Let me look at you, Vanessa," he said, and he stood back to look at me in my black knit dress.

He looked handsome, gray-haired and distinguished, with a glow of health in his sun-browned skin. He and Aunt Melissa were back from a trip around the world. When I was little, I used to read Uncle Charles's weekly letter from Washington to Grandpa Nye, and in the letters Cordell Hull used to ask Uncle Charles how Grandpa Nye was and send him his regards. That made me think we must be important.

"It's so nice to see you, Aunt Melissa," I said. I looked into her eyes until I was embarrassed. That always happened with Aunt Melissa because she was loving and very shy, so we gazed fondly into each other's eyes and neither of us could think of what to say. When she spoke, she chose her words with care, and sometimes she stammered.

"How is Papa?" Uncle Charles asked Daddy.

"He has failed considerably since you saw him, Charles," Daddy said, and he turned away.

"Poor Papa," Uncle Charles said. "He always wanted to . . ."

I got a drink of Hudson Bay scotch from Daddy and went to stand by the fire near Uncle Edward, who had the same physical strength that was in Grandpa Nye in my early memories of him. For a moment I had the sense of warm well-being I used to have in Grandpa Nye's library, sitting in one of the child's chairs by the fire, listening to the men talk. Uncle Edward was taller than Daddy or Uncle Charles and larger boned; his voice was louder, and he took things easier. His face was wide and strong-boned and very handsome.

"Edward has been drinking too much since Kate died," Daddy told me earlier. "I'm worried about him." Uncle Edward's gray eyes had a flaming, haunted look, and his mouth looked worn with his grief.

Now Daddy brought Uncle Edward a drink. "Here's a good stiff highball, Edward," he said, and

Uncle Edward, gesturing in the Nye fashion, told Daddy the problems he had had getting an actual piece—weighing several tons—of the Rock of Gibraltar installed in his back yard on the shore of Lake Ontario. That prompted Daddy to tell Uncle Edward—*sotto voce*, so Janice wouldn't hear—the story of how he got the petrified log from Grandpa Nye's front lawn moved out to Glendale one Saturday morning in the spring after Janice had casually told him that she'd given the log to Mr. Jerry James, the real-estate agent who had sold her the house in Indian Hill.

"Papa told me years ago that he was giving it to me," Daddy said. "So I phoned Natorp to come to Avondale on an urgent basis with their big tree-moving trunk. They arrived in an hour, backed up the truck, and ran out the big crane. Wrapping the log in burlap and boards, they secured chains around it and hoisted it up and slid it back onto the truck bed and off to Glendale where it was dropped on the ground here behind the drive." Daddy and Uncle Edward stepped outside to have a look at the petrified log.

Edie came over to me. "Charles is very upset," she said in her low voice. "I've never seen him so upset.

He stopped to see Grandpa Nye on his way home from the office, and—"

Daddy and Uncle Edward joined us. Daddy said, "It was around 1910 that Papa's friend Mr. Gardener first heard of the Petrified Forest in Arizona. He went out to Arizona to see just what it was all about, and in his usual expansive fashion he bought an entire flat-car load to be shipped to his lumberyard in Cincinnati. After it was unloaded, he wondered just what to do with it. Moving those two-ton objects always was a problem. Papa induced him to give a petrified log to the Museum of Natural History, one to the Art Museum, and one to the Public Library. And, of course, Papa got the one for his front lawn. . . ."

Uncle Charles bent down and said to Amy in the deep, formal voice he used to address children, "You are a fine specimen, Amy Marston Dunlap." He stood up. "This child of yours is a fine specimen, Lisa," he said, and Lisa laughed, pleased.

When Charles came in, he looked ashen. "What can I get you, Charles?" Daddy asked.

Charles wanted a martini. I got another drink of scotch.

"Slow down, Vanessa," Mama said loudly from across the room.

221

Black rage went through me. "Mama!" I said.

Charles and I drifted through the hall and into the dining room, where we stood in front of the corner case. "What happened?" I said. I looked up at Charles. He was much taller than I, and he had a thick, athletic build. Everything about his dark, handsome face was (like mine) a little curly—his short black hair, his long nose, his thick mouth, his smile, his chin. Usually his brown eyes were bright with tenderness and amusement, but now he was looking blankly into the corner case.

"I stopped by to see Grandpa Nye on my way home from town and Aunt Janice wasn't there," he said. Charles spoke in a voice so deep it sometimes seemed to rub against sandpaper, and he had a warm Ohio-Princeton twang. "When I walked in, Grandpa Nye said, 'Help me to dress, Charles, I'm not going to spend another night in here.' He spoke very clearly."

"Oh, Charles," I said.

"I hate myself," Charles said. "I said he should stay in the hospital until he got well. His voice was hollow, but very clear. He said, 'I want to go home.' He said, 'I want to go down to the river.' I didn't answer him. *I didn't answer him*, Vanessa. Then he asked

222

when Edie would be delivered." Charles's voice broke. In a moment he said in a steadied voice, "And he asked about the library building."

Daddy and Edie came into the dining room. "You two look exactly like brother and sister," Edie said. She stood on tiptoe and kissed Charles.

I looked down into a low shelf of the corner case and saw some bones and a skull back in the corner. "Oh, Daddy, where did you get that skull?" I asked. "I never saw it before."

"It's an Indian skull," Daddy said. "My brother Joab retrieved it. I remember the day very well." His eyes lighted up, and he smiled his intricate, wonderful smile, and began, "Papa, of course, was always interested in Indians, and by the time I was a small boy my older brothers had become fascinated. We used to make extensive excursions in search of Indian artifacts. Sometimes we went to North Bend to Fort Hill, the mound there on the backbone of a great hill to the west of where the Harrison farm was. William Henry Harrison was the first to discover Fort Hill and he wrote about it in his *Discourse on the Aborigines of the Valley of the Ohio*, which Papa greatly admired as a literary work. Of course, while we were there, we always visited General Harrison's tomb on a knoll overlooking the Ohio. The whole place was over-grown with weeds, shrubs, and unkempt trees. I re-call Papa endeavoring around 1910 to get the state or federal government to clean up the place and pre-serve the tomb and monument, but it was many years before anything was done. Papa was always inter-ested in Harrison, you know, but it was only after he retired from business that he was able to devote him-self to writing his biography.

"Frequently we walked to Norwood to search around the old Indian mound near the water tower. In the early nineteen-hundreds these areas had not been picked over and we often came home with five or six arrowheads and other interesting miscellany. Even in the Bloody Run Valley behind our house, be-fore the sewer was built, and long before the Victory Parkway was put in, we found fine pickings of Indian relics. But the big event was one Saturday afternoon in 1906. A telephone call came from Leonard Gar-rison in Terrace Park to Edward, saying that in the new sand-and-gravel-pit diggings they had just unearthed an Indian burial ground—come quick! That both families had telephones was unique, and that one could get from the northeast end of Avondale to Terrace Park in half an hour is still something to figure out. My mother called the stables, and in a few minutes a carriage was over, which dashed to the Montgomery Pike in Norwood and the terminus of the Swingline Traction. Once aboard, the traction zoomed off through Oakley, Madisonville, Madeira, and through a slot down a creek bed through Indian Hill right into Terrace Park. The Garrisons were at the station. By foot we proceeded. Joab carried me part of the way on his shoulders. And there was the excavation! I distinctly recall the bones, skulls, pottery, and beads dropping from the exposed side of the burial place, and how with unrestrained ghoulish delight Charles and Joab each retrieved a skull. Edward retrieved a nice shoulder and forearm. A few thighbones and some ribs were accumulated. A further skull with an arrowhead imbedded in it was found. A few fingers, toes, and miscellaneous pieces including teeth from broken jaws. I don't recall much in the way of beads and pottery from that grave robbery. I think the Nyes and the Garrisons were just in a hurry to collect before the find was well-known. Also there was the hurry to get home in view of the Saturday afternoon traction schedule and the problem of walking from Norwood to Avondale with the gruesome loot. There was to be no carriage. But all got safely home. I think this skull is the one Joab retrieved. Your father, Charles, has, I believe, the skull with the arrowhead imbedded in it somewhere in his house in Washington."

Charles grinned, pleased. He loved Daddy's stories.

Uncle Charles came to the door of the dining room. "Morgan," he said in a serious tone, "there is something I would like to discuss with you and Edward." The three tall brothers went into the study and shut the door. They behaved toward each other with the most perfect formal brotherly politeness, but underneath, Daddy was often in a rage over Uncle Charles and his habits. "I hate my brother Charles," I heard him say once to someone at a cocktail party. When Daddy was little, Uncles Charles used to put a napkin over his head so he wouldn't have to watch Daddy eat. "Charles always said 'Mine!'" Daddy told me once, and he imitated him, shouting in an ugly way, "Mine! Mine!"

I'd never heard Uncle Edward criticized for anything except for not being on time and for having too many children. He had eight.

"I'll get another martini," Charles said darkly. He was still ashen.

I stared a moment into the corner case at one of the scarabs and remembered, long ago when we were children at Grandpa Nye's, Uncle Andrew said, "In ancient Egypt when the Pharaoh died, the scarab carried his soul to the sun. The scarab was the symbol of death and resurrection, for it crawled into a ball of dung to lay its eggs, and later out flew a beetle with gossamer wings."

We went back to the living room, where Lisa was taking Amy around to say good night. Mama's hands looked stiff and old on Amy's back, as if she didn't know how to hug her really. "I didn't hold you when you were little, or pick you up when you cried," Mama said once. "You weren't meant to in those days."

When Aunt Aggie bent down to kiss Amy good night, she said tenderly, shaking her head a bit, "Good night, little Vanesser."

I felt like crying. On the stairs Lisa said, "Mama's called her Vanessa, too. I think she reminds them of you when you were little."

We went into Lisa's old room. In there it was cold and a little dark and it smelled of wallpaper the way it always did. Amy lay on her bed looking voluptuously down at herself. Lisa put on her faded yellow pajama bottoms with feet.

The phone rang. Grandpa Nye, I wondered, thinking of him alone in his hospital room, staring wildly. Daddy called up from downstairs, "Lisa, long distance for you."

"Stewart," Lisa said, pleased. She went into Mama and Daddy's room and shut the door.

"Amy, shall I put on your pajama tops?" I asked.

She sat up without a word and put her arms up over her head. "There," I said, and I began snapping the tops to the bottoms. Her hand with its baby fat and its delicate flower-petal quality reached out to my face. "Amy," I said.

"Vanessa," she said. Then we sat side by side on the edge of the bed, talking. "There was a fire," she said. "My daddy took me."

"Really?" I said.

"Yes," she said, nodding her head. "Long ago."

She became exuberant, telling me different things—how Ralph, her dog, threw up on the rug, how she saw a cow in the road, she did, how she weeweed in the water in Maine. As she talked, she moved her arms, her hands, just the way Daddy did when he talked expansively. It was the same gesture that Grandpa Nye used, that I used, that Uncle Edward used, carried in our blood down through the first DeGolyer who walked in the American forest.

When Lisa came back, we tucked her in. "Good night, sleep tight, sweet dreams," we said. "Sleep tight, sweet dreams," Amy said.

"She'll be up again, but that's a start," Lisa said, drawing the door halfway shut.

"She's so lovely, Lisa," I said. "I can't get over it. I know I'll always love her."

"It's not so easy when you're the mother," Lisa said. We went into the bathroom to comb our hair and fix our lipstick. "When she was little and I was nursing her, she wouldn't get enough, and then she'd cry. She wouldn't stop crying. And I *hated* her for it, Vanessa. You don't know what that's like," she said furiously. "I'll be better next time. You always are. Oh, Vanessa, I didn't tell you, I'm pregnant! I wanted to tell Stewart first. I already feel different."

"Oh, Lisa," I said lovingly, but a wave of uneasiness went through my body.

"Stewart's so pleased with himself," she said. "I told him on the phone just now."

I hugged her. My sister, I thought. For a moment I

felt all the tenderness of her, her soft arms, her warm body, as if the hardness in her were not real.

"If he's a boy, we're going to name him after Daddy," Lisa said. "Just think, Vanessa, right now he is a tiny fish."

"And his *heart* is beating," I said.

"Amy's like you," Lisa said. "I think that's part of my problem with her. I used to resent you so, Vanessa. I hated you. And I never faced it until I got married and Stewart pointed it out to me."

"Lisa!" I was horribly hurt.

"Vanessa," she said, "do you remember when we were little the time we had oyster stew for lunch at Grandmother Marston's, and you and I didn't want to eat ours, and Daddy found the pearl in one of his oysters and he said whoever finished first would win the pearl, and you won the pearl . . ."

"No, Lisa, *you* won the pearl," I said.

"Oh, no, Vanessa, *you* won the pearl. And I was so *mad* you won it I went upstairs and took Uncle Virgil's straight razor and cut half way through his exercising belt. Then they asked me if I'd done it and I said I hadn't, and I knew they knew I was lying. I went outside into Grandmother Marston's wild flower garden. Do you remember? The dark garden across the drive on the side by the castle. There were bleeding hearts. I was crying. I remember the bleeding hearts."

"Then I must have won it," I said. "But then I lost it."

"I couldn't have stood it if you hadn't, Vanessa," she said.

In my mind I groped, trying to remember, but I got no further than seeing the pearl in my hand and the white bureau in the guest room where I was going to put the pearl so I wouldn't lose it.

We were standing at the top of the stairs. I took hold of the bannister to go down.

In the dining room the candles were lit. The room was soft and warm. The silver and glasses glowed on the table, and the fruit, piled high in the bowl in the center of the table, gleamed. Uncle Charles's eyes looked sad again; I put my arm around him and we smiled at each other.

On the mantelpiece the candles in the brass candlesticks were lit and the candlelight shone in the holly and mistletoe and in the smooth gold frame around the painting of trunks of trees done by Daddy's Great-Aunt Kate DeGolyer, the one he despised. The tree trunks receded into the dark forest primeval.

"Aunt Isabel, it looks as if you made a Druid altar," Charles said.

We took our places at the table, and Daddy asked Uncle Charles to say grace. We bowed our heads and Uncle Charles said, "Our Heavenly Father, we thank Thee for all the blessings of the past; we put our trust in Thee for the future; and ask that our strengths may ever be used as Thou wouldst have it. Amen."

Eugenie brought in the turkey. "A magnificent bird!" Aunt Aggie said, and Daddy started to carve. "Morgan is a superior carver," Mama said to Uncle Edward on her right. Eugenie came round with silver bowls of mashed potatoes and asparagus.

"Papa wrote that grace," Uncle Charles said to me, "when he was a young man in the days when a young man, invited out to supper, might be asked to say grace."

"Is that what he was always saying?" I said.

"Yes," Uncle Charles said. "He said it too fast."

"I never heard a word of it except 'Amen,'" I said, thinking of Grandpa Nye unfolding his wrinkled, leathery hands and pouring the wine, as Daddy now did, taking a sip from the bit in his glass. Lisa and I looked anxiously at each other—it was a bottle of Grandpa Nye's red—but it was good. We smiled, relieved.

With one of the honey-colored goblets from Grandpa Nye's house, Daddy stood now to propose the first toast. He faltered a moment, and then he said, "Let us drink to affection between people and to great education for children."

"Ah," said Uncle Edward. "Sour, potent, and infinitely invigorating."

The wine had the taste I loved in red wine—like the taste of cool forest mud, I thought.

"Papa always mixed the wild fox grapes from the banks of the Ohio in with cultivated grapes," Uncle Charles said. "'The wild gifts of God,' his friend Clark B. Firestone used to say."

Uncle Charles said, "Let us drink to those of us who cannot be with us tonight."

"Let us drink to your father," Aunt Janice said, nodding her china-blue eyes to Daddy and Uncle Charles and Uncle Edward.

"Let us drink to his wine!" Aunt Aggie said uproariously.

"It is the equal of the finest French wines," Uncle Charles said.

"Calvin died a week ago today," Aunt Janice said to Aunt Melissa, who was sitting next to her. "He died on his seventeenth birthday. He was one hundred and nineteen dog-years old."

I looked across at Charles. He sat there quietly, taking part in the dinner, but I knew that under the table his leg was jittering wildly.

Mama was talking to Uncle Edward on her right. "I have no memory at all, but Morgan has the world's most remarkable memory," she said.

Aunt Melissa said quietly, "All the Nyes have remarkable memories."

"Kate used to say—" Uncle Edward began, but Aunt Janice interrupted him and said, "Nate remembered whatever he *wanted* to remember." She giggled.

"It was often highly inaccurate," Mama said.

"Mama!" I said. We're talking about him as if he were already dead, I thought.

"I remember things that happened when I was two," Uncle Charles said, "but my earliest memory of an event outside the house was during the Pullman Strike when Grover Cleveland called out the troops to let the mails go through."

"That was in 1892," Charles said tentatively.

"Eighteen ninety-four," Uncle Charles said sternly, but he looked at his son with respect.

"My earliest memory of an event outside the house was the assassination of McKinley," Uncle Edward said. "I remember there was some question about whether to call off the Autumn Festival that year. It was decided that the festival would go on, but we would wear black bands for mourning. There's a picture—I wonder where it is—of us all in our decorated pony cart in front of the house, the black bands on our arms. Your father isn't in the picture, Lisa and Vanessa. He was still a babe in arms. He hadn't even been named yet. Did you know that he had no name for more than a year? We called him Baby. Mama wanted to name him Reginald or one of those names in fashion then, but Papa wanted to name him after Morgan Burke, who had no children of his own."

Uncle Edward settled back in his chair and gestured. "Why, I recall the day Morgan was born. It was a complete surprise. We were sent off to school with sandwiches for lunch, and on the way home after school, we met a maid who said, Hurry home, we had a baby brother. It was a complete surprise. That started a discussion in our gang about how babies came to be. At age nine it was a fascinating subject."

"It was no surprise to *me*," Uncle Charles said. "Good Lord, man!"

We all laughed.

"I remember the night Mark Twain died," Daddy said. "The *Enquirer* telephoned Papa for comment, and Papa stood back and delivered his eulogy, bellowing into the phone. It appeared on the front page in the morning."

"Papa could do that sort of thing right off the cuff," Daddy said to Edie. "When he was a young man and he needed money, why he'd just hire a hall and talk."

Lisa said, "I remember, Daddy, it was September, and our house was being remodeled, and we were staying at Grandmother Marston's. You were upstairs and we were down in the living room and we heard on the radio that the Germans and Russians had invaded Poland. I went running upstairs to tell you, and you were standing there in the guest room, and when I told you, you moved your arm in a horrible way, slapping it down against your leg. I thought you were mad at me for telling you."

I could remember Mama saying in the spring before that, "Today, girls, write down in your diaries: 'Today Daddy opened his office—Morgan Burke Nye, Foreign Patents & Trademarks.'"

The plates were cleared. Mama brought a bowl of nuts from the sideboard, and Eugenie brought in a platter of cheeses. Coffee was served, and then liqueurs. We continued to eat fruit. Mama recalled the time when, after Christmas dinner, Charles ate eight bananas. "*Eight* bananas," she repeated.

"Uncle Charles," I said, "do you remember you were going to tell me the story of the time Cousin Cato ate 99 bananas."

He smiled. "Another time," he said.

After dinner I went out to the kitchen to thank Eugenie. "How was your grandfather today?" Eugenie asked.

"Oh, Eugenie," I said unhappily. "Look, it's snowing." I opened the back door and stepped out. I put my hands out to catch the soft flakes, and I listened to the sweet quiet, and I thought, Down on the river at North Bend a steamboat whistles in the snowy night to honor, as it passes, General Harrison in his grave there in the hills. And far to the north in the frozen silence of the forest the moon is shining on the snow-covered Lake of Everlasting Waters.

When I went back into the dining room, Daddy and Charles had got the magic mirrors out of the corner case. The room was dark except for the light from the corner case, which Daddy and Charles were trying to catch so it would reflect on the ceiling.

"Papa used to take these out after dinner when we had a party, and just like that," Daddy said, snapping his finger and thumb, "the Empress of Japan appeared on the ceiling."

Everyone was drinking cognac in the dark room and talking. Daddy and Charles were tilting the mirrors this way and that, moving them up and down, trying to focus the images in the blurred circles of light in the ceiling.

"Papa did it with a flourish, as if he were a magician," Uncle Charles said.

I touched Lisa on the arm. "It's snowing," I said.

"Oh, Vanessa," Mama said, "did Lisa tell you what Amy said last year when she saw her first snow? She went up to the window. 'Mew,' she said, 'Mew.'" Mama went off across the room to tell Aunt Melissa.

And suddenly there was the Empress of Japan in her garden! And there was the Emperor! We all clapped. "A toast to the magicians," Aunt Aggie said.

Just then the phone rang. The circles of light vanished from the ceiling, and Daddy went rapidly to the phone.

He put down the phone. "Papa is dead," Daddy said in a strange voice, looking at the wall. I was afraid he was going to cry. But he turned toward us and, steadying his voice, he said, "Papa is dead."